To Marcie —

Thanks for teaching me to love the sound of language. Here's another Lexington — mythic, dark, but in the end, transcendent.

With deep affection,
Johnny Payne
November 1996

OTHER WORK BY JOHNNY PAYNE

The Ambassador's Son
A Novella

Voice & Style

Conquest of the New Word:
Experimental Fiction & Translation in the Americas

The Devil in Disputanta
A Musical Play in Three Acts

CHALK LAKE
A Novel

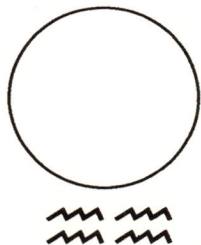

Johnny Payne

Limited Editions Press
Lubbock, Texas
1996

Copyright©1996 by Johnny Payne

All rights reserved. No part of this book may be reproduced by any means and in any form whatsoever without written permission from the publisher, except for brief quotations embodied in literary articles or reviews. For information, please address:

Limited Editions Press
2003 16th Street
Lubbock, TX 79401-4609

All characters and geographical settings in this book are fictitious, and any resemblance to actual locales or to any persons, living or dead, is purely coincidental.

Library of Congress Cataloging-in-Publication Data
Johnny Payne, 1958-
Chalk Lake: a novel / Johnny Payne.
  p.   cm.
ISBN 0-9647515-2-6 (hardcover). — ISBN 0-9647515-1-8 (pbk.)
1. Pregnant women—Kentucky—Fiction. 2. Young women—Kentucky— Fiction
  3. Farm life—Kentucky—Fiction   I. Title.
          PS3566.A9375C43   1996
813'.54—dc20   96-19325
                                                       CIP
First Edition

ISBN 0-9647515-2-6 (hardcover)
ISBN 0-9647515-1-8 (paperback)

Printed in the United States of America by Thomson-Shore, Dexter, MI

To H. G. and Clayton

I
♒

∿∿
∿∿

And am I born to die
to lay this body down
and must my trembling spirit fly
into a world unknown

A land of deepest shade
unpierced by human thought
that dreary region of the dead
where all things are forgot

—Appalachian hymn

≈   Serena scrambled down the sloping bank overgrown with cattails. In the dark, they looked like caterpillars come out from hiding places to feed on stalks. Ferns brushed against her legs and sprang back into place. There was probably poison oak scattered among the ground cover, but she was immune to it. Kelsey, with her redhead's copious freckles and sensitive skin, was the one who got rashes and food allergies, the one who had to be rushed to an emergency room for cortisone once when she'd stumbled into a patch of poison ivy down at the Red River Gorge. There had been pustules inside Kelsey's eyelids, in her vagina, between her toes. Serena could stick the reddish-green leaves in her mouth, chew them up and swallow them, and had done so as a child to freak out Kelsey.

Feeling her way past the ground cover with her bare feet, she found the marshy edge where the water began. This was how her parents' Irish mutthound favored going in. He always swam with her in the mornings when she came for a visit. The algae grew copious and mossy as she waded in deeper. It closed around her body. At first, its slime unnerved her, but then it seemed almost a comfort, a clingy garment she had tossed aside when the weather turned sharp the previous season, and now she was re-encountering it, having forgotten in the meantime it existed.

Her sluggish movements made her realize she was still a little drunk from the wine at dinner. She shivered, realizing what she had come down here for, what she had failed to do. It had only been a half-conscious notion. Halfhearted, even. The dock was rotting, and her parents, in the five years they'd lived on Chalk Lake, had never gotten around to rebuilding it or even to hanging an aluminum ladder so that visitors could climb down. It might have taken some deliberate effort to carry out her notion, since even in pure darkness, she knew where the submerged logs and shallows lay. But after standing for a long time at the edge of the dock, she'd decided to skinny dip instead.

CHALK LAKE ~

She hadn't gone skinny dipping in more than a year. That fact came over her with almost as much of a shock as the pocket of cold water. There hadn't been anywhere to do it living on the edge of Hell's Kitchen. Or sure, there was doubtless someplace in or around New York where you could, but she hadn't learned her way around well enough yet to discover a swimming hole. Kelsey was too busy waiting tables and rehearsing at the theater co-op to go out exploring with her, and Skip was always on tour with the flamenco company, in some college town.

She frog-kicked her way out to the deeper water, and the algae slid away from her limbs. Her body felt boyish. She could have done some smooth, blind strokes, flaunting her prowess to herself, but all she wanted was to get out toward the middle and tread water. In the dark, even a little man-made lake like this felt immense once you moved a certain distance from the shore's outline. The lake had been excavated by a rich guy from Mt. Sterling, Colonel something or other, back in the fifties, who'd built a hunting lodge out here for himself and his buddies, and wanted to have a big ol' fish pond handy. He was a Kentucky Colonel, not a real one, one of those honorary By Decree of the Commonwealth piece of paper things. He was a fake and the lake was a fake. But tonight, this body of water seemed as old and real as anything she'd ever inhabited. Fireflies provided the only flashes of light. She'd never seen so many of them. They hovered over the water so thick and close that the celestial sphere seemed to have lowered into a canopy just above the water's surface, solely for her pleasure. It was high summer. Tree frogs plunked a catgut sound, and crickets throbbed.

Her father would have thrown a fit if he'd known she was out here swimming alone past midnight. He understood perfectly well that she was competent and strong, she'd always been a tomboy. But since he'd started getting that game leg, it made him nervous to watch people swimming in the lake, even in the daytime and close to the dock. Luckily for her, the next-door neighbor, who used his cabin only as an occasional summer place, had offered to let Serena stay in it for her first couple of days. So her father would be none the wiser. She floated on her back and let a long sigh shudder through her. This was the most relaxed she'd felt in a long time. Things in New York hadn't worked out quite the way she'd expected. A hard city like that was fine for somebody like Kelsey, who'd gone up there straight out of high school and learned right off to give tart responses to people when they deserved it, instead of always internalizing and feeling she was somehow to blame. She also had a burning sense of mission. Kelsey's talents in life were easily discernible, unambiguous, and even though she'd spent six years so far trying to break in as an actress with nothing palpable to show for it except once getting her picture in a *Redbook* spread on teen fashion, you still always had the sense that she was eventually going to succeed, and that even if she didn't, it would be a case of gross cosmic injustice because her talent was so achingly clear.

Serena, on the other hand, couldn't say what her talent was. There were a lot of things she did passably well, like raising houseplants, getting sick ones with mites or fungus to recover, making pottery. Or calling production as a backstage manager, but that was a stopgap really, and besides, even people in technical theater, the nuts and bolts end of things, mostly had to resign themselves to working for free in New York. She was only willing to do that for so long. Theater wasn't a religion for her like it was for Kelsey. If she was honest with herself, what she mostly enjoyed were the parties, getting to hang out with bohemian people who made constant witty remarks and had a kind of happy cynicism and flamboyance about them.

Kelsey couldn't stand that side of things. She would smoke dope with their crowd just to be sociable, and she'd been drinking a little harder lately than she should, but without any gaiety. When Kelsey drank, she did it purposefully, the way she did everything, and wouldn't stop until she'd achieved the state of numbness she'd established as her goal. It was a project, like everything in her life. Without ever getting self-righteous about it, she was a purist. Kelsey was the best actress Serena knew, and the least theatrical person. Because of her temperament, their mutual theater friends tended wrongly to think of Serena as one of their own, and Kelsey as the outsider. A girl named Devra—"That's Devra with a vee"—was always saying to Kelsey, in an unaccountably throaty voice, "You're so down to earth. You're so lucky to have been raised in Kentucky." Kelsey would turn to her and say, "Have you ever been to Kentucky?" "No." "Then what the fuck are you talking about?" That ended the conversation, until the next time.

If it hadn't been for the fact that Kelsey already long since had established residence and rent-control rights in that apartment in Hell's Kitchen and had invited Serena to share digs with her, Serena probably never would have made the trip. The best job she'd had was as a full-time nanny, for a whole year, with paid vacation and benefits. The kids called her Aunt Serena, and the parents were always asking her to stay on for dinner, they would order something in.

Then she felt compelled to quit because things were starting to get complicated between her and the father. Not that they had actually done anything, but he was starting to hit on her in small ways, dropping in at home unexpectedly at mid-morning for some tax document he'd supposedly forgotten. It was always that way with her and men. She seemed to emit a constant, low-grade sexuality that drew them, and in this case she was attracted to the man too. The fact that he was married hadn't stopped her. Her hesitation had more to do with her working as a nanny. She couldn't abide the thought of fornicating like some lusty, wicked servant girl in a Restoration play, the kind of girl that Kelsey, who was always cast as the character actor, never as the heroine, used to portray when she was still studying at the Academy.

There were a lot of things Serena was willing to be, while casting around for a more permanent identity, but a leering wench wasn't one of them. Even without the sexual undertones, there was something depressing about raising another couple's glowing, perfect kids. So she stopped doing it. Since she'd gotten involved with Skip, she'd used his career as a flamenco dancer as an excuse for staying. But the fact was, Skip spent only three or four months out of the year in New York, while the company rehearsed. He was always in Des Moines, or Austin, or even Louisville.

As she dove down under the surface, a root caught her ankle for a second, the kind of sharp, unexpected tug that might have put a less experienced swimmer into a panic. A stray tendril, panic, death. The sequence was that simple. Serena shook the root off with nonchalance. She reflected almost wistfully that if she started to drown, no one could possibly reach her in time to save her. Navigating underwater, she encountered still more tangles of fibers. Vegetable matter was slowly taking over the lake. Colonel Whatsisname obviously hadn't dug it deep enough. Her father said the Lake Association had tried everything, including having mesh wire laid along the entire bottom, but after a couple of years, the algae just pierced the wire and grew back up again.

She waded back onto the bank. She'd mislaid her clothes, but it didn't matter. She would get them tomorrow. If a car happened to cruise by as she was crossing the service road, the driver, coming upon her flesh pale in the headlights, would have to conclude that he had seen the ghost of a woman drowned by her lover, the way it always happened in those scandalous mountain ballads that her grandfather loved to sing. Tresses wrapped around the throat, and the life slowly choked out. The beloved would weep for mercy, but the lover, unmoved, only pulled the harder to stop her pleading. Later, he would hang by a rope for his sins. The murdered woman's soul would wander forever and always, a-sorrowing and a-grieving. The mere thought of it gave her goosebumps. Serena smiled to herself in the dark, and walked back uphill among the cattails.

In the morning, not too early, her mother called over to the borrowed cabin on the phone to tell her she had breakfast on. The sun rose above the tops of the trees across the lake as Serena shambled next door, slightly hungover. The Canadian geese had long since quieted their dawn honking—a racket that her father referred to as Chalk Lake's rush hour. The geese drifted in a group toward the footbridge, with two stragglers. She must have been sleeping extra soundly that she hadn't heard the geese. Perhaps because the lake was so small, they didn't swim so much as let themselves be pulled along by the subtle currents. It was odd that of all the lakes in the country they could have chosen to adopt, they'd settled on this modest one.

As she opened the screen, the Irish mutthound appeared out of nowhere, covered with burrs, and bolted through the doorway, ears down, almost knocking her over. Her parents' art collection was crowded along the walls of their cabin, taking up most of the space. Paintings, houseplants, and strays were her mother's three collector's passions. She had the largest jade plant in captivity, its fleshy lobes glossy and thriving even in winter, and the groaning of one superannuated shaggy beast or another could always be heard beneath the bed. The cabin, built for seasonal use, was barely big enough for her parents, even if you included the glassed-in sun porch, which in any case had been turned into a virtual greenhouse by her mother.

But at least Carson and Josie had finally been able to scrape together enough money for a down payment on something instead of renting apartments for the rest of their lives. The cabin was theirs, or would be someday. They had first driven up to it at night, and seeing only its silhouette, Josie had turned to Carson in the pitch black and said yes, she wanted it. For many years, Serena's father's wages as dairy manager at the grocery simply hadn't stretched very far, but even when he started making a regular minister's salary and moonlighting at the grocery, there had been children's theater, Kelsey's braces and ballet lessons, the two girls' obscenely large wardrobes in high school, and the summer after their respective sophomore years, the six-nation European tour in the youth orchestra that her mother had insisted each of the girls should take.

Serena hadn't protested, but now she wondered at the extravagance of it. Her bowing technique could have been excellent, according to the orchestra leader and chaperone, if only she'd expended a little effort. But playing the violin, especially in a recital, made her so tense the bow would jump on the strings. Breathe, Serena, breathe, her teacher kept telling her. But she couldn't breathe. He was from Poland, and a true virtuoso. He should have been teaching at a high-powered conservatory, but he had ten children to support, so he had chosen to live in a smaller town in a bigger house, teaching at the state university and giving private lessons on the side. He rode an ancient bicycle to work, one with a bell on the handlebars, his violin case and sheet music laid in the wire basket. He'd wanted to make her into a project, but each time he left, she would go into the bathroom, lock the door, and lie on her side in the dry tub with the shower curtain drawn, trying to catch her breath.

At the time, she kept telling everyone that she planned to play the fiddle in a bluegrass band, and so didn't have any use for classical music. Mostly what she remembered from the European tour was smoking hashish that tasted like cough drops and burnt cork in somebody's hotel room in Amsterdam, then strolling along the avenue of the red light district with a group of the boys to look over the prostitutes displayed in the windows. She had eyed the women on their high stools, legs apart. What amazed her was not so much that the women would have sex for pay, but that they could bear to display themselves to passersby in that way. It was like filing by an open casket, gawking at the rouge and lipstick that had been too thickly applied, to create the illusion of vitality.

Then, in Munich, she'd slept under a featherbed for the first time, with a trumpeter, the orchestra leader's son. Her parents probably had taken out a loan for that trip, and perhaps they were still paying it off. She'd tried to dissuade them from sending her, but they wanted her to have it as a life experience. Once the trip was over, she'd never picked up a violin again. After the two girls moved to New York, there had been countless care packages, containing everything from country ham to spermicide, and in the last couple of years, her parents had also been contributing on a regular basis to help stage the plays of Kelsey's fledgling playwright boyfriend.

Serena sat down at the kitchen table and stubbed out her first cigarette of the day. She kept giving them up, but never for long. In one of her parents' storage trunks, she'd found a halter top and bell bottoms. She'd bought them in high school, and they still fit. Well, the top did anyway; her bust, more's the pity, never seemed to grow, even when she was on the pill. But she was starting to get a little broad in the beam, like her mother. Even Kelsey, the waif, had hips on her. Serena exhaled the last mouthful of smoke, feet tucked beneath her in the chair.

Her mother was cooking breakfast. She had a weakness for her mother's gravy. Josie made it without lumps, and she knew without measuring exactly how much pepper should go in. It was obvious she was trying to avoid asking Serena what had prompted the call to her parents in the middle of the night, only a few days ago, announcing that she was coming to Kentucky. No, nothing was wrong, she just had to get out of New York for a while. It was a very tense city, and she needed someplace quiet, without garbage trucks compacting all night long, someplace where she could think about things. Josie swept the excess flour into a paper sack, making a show of it. Nothing to worry about, a summer vacation. She poured the gravy onto two fat biscuits and set that portion of the plate on the table directly in front of Serena, close enough that she could feel as well as smell the rising steam. The aroma brought tears to her eyes.

"Those green apples aren't any good, but I cooked them up anyway. Last summer, the Purcells from church gave us the juiciest, crispest winesaps you could ever hope to lay your mouth on. Out of their orchard."

"They taste perfect, mom." Chewing each bite slowly, she let it dissolve in her mouth.

"I wish I had some of those winesaps instead of these mealy whatever they are from the grocery store. They cost a dollar forty-nine a pound and they don't have any flavor. I doubt we're going to have another Indian summer like last year. I don't know what's taking your father so long. All I asked him to pick up was a can of shortening and some filtered water in town, but he finds somebody he knows in every single aisle and spends two hours chewing the fat. Once a preacher gets to talking, there's no shutting him up."

Josie had never learned to drive, and so Carson was always off on some errand or other, when he wasn't tending to his congregation. After getting a good look at the jalopy he'd been driving, the church members had wisely chipped in and given him a used car, a road hog much too wide for the county roads with their blind curves and raised, crumbling asphalt without shoulders. But it got him around, with a powerful, seemingly immortal engine, and the local drivers had learned to give Carson a wide berth. Don't give it a name, Dad, she had told him the first time she saw the road hog. As soon as you christen your cars, they start to die.

Having served Serena, Josie allowed herself to sit down for a moment. As brassy as she could be at times, she yet clung to the ancient mountain habit of eating at the second table, even if there was only one other person besides herself to be served. More often than not, she took her meals standing up at the counter.

Josie pressed a hot coffee cup to one side of her nose, and rested it at the sinus cavity for a few seconds. The operation she'd had several years ago to relieve her congestion had only made her breathing more laborious, and though she was allergic to both dogs and cats, she insisted on keeping the house full of them. No matter how many ailments Josie contracted, bone spurs, gallstones, arthritis, she could always find some human or animal sicker than herself to attend to. From time to time she would complain about her ailments, but not as though she expected anyone to do anything about them. She still traveled to Lexington twice a month to visit in the nursing home with her painter friend Therese, who'd contracted Alzheimer's years ago. She'd nursed her own mother through a long bout of diabetes, brought her up to the cabin from her house in Middlesboro to live with them, bought her a recliner with electric controls, administered the insulin, kept watch over her day and night until she'd passed away.

Now Carson had cancer. He'd been diagnosed with multiple myeloma a year ago, over and above his bad leg, but he never seemed the least bit blue about his condition. He had a strong and quiet faith in God, not one he boasted about but simply exuded. After the initial numbness, her mother had accommodated to the idea as well. Josie had always said her worst fear in life was not to die, but to outlive all the people she cared about. Carson hadn't wanted to take the oral chemotherapy at first, not out of fear but just on principle, but Josie pointed her finger at him and said, "If you have to eat horseshit to get well, you'll eat horseshit. Now, that's all I'm going to say about it." And once he made his peace with the idea, he became the model patient. The doctors had given him as few as three years to live, as many as twelve. But he was the kind who would live beyond the maximum expectations, because of his innate optimism. He was one of those who would be cited as anecdotal evidence of the power of positive thinking and the miracle of modern medicine.

What did Serena have to complain about? She couldn't even name her fears. She'd tried to carry on the nurturing and stoical tradition of her mother, of her forebears, of her Appalachian stock, by tending to friends in crisis rather than thinking so much about the nature of her own problems. Over time she'd learned about massage and therapeutic touch, and by rubbing her hands together and bringing up the chakra within herself, she had healed the pain of dozens of people. She never charged them for it, either, and as a result her friends and acquaintances called on her often and around the clock.

Now a part of her wanted Josie all to herself. She had an intense urge to fling her arms around her mother and cry out *Mommy, Mommy,* but she had no idea what words would come after that. There really wasn't anything to be saved from. Her mother had enough to deal with without Serena going into some kind of infantile state, so she would do her best to stay levelheaded and cool, in the style of Kelsey. There was nothing wrong with stating a proposal, as long as she was mature about it. "Josie, I've been thinking that I might stay on here in Kentucky for a while."

"Nothing wrong with that. You said on the phone you needed a break from New York. It's a mean city."

"Yes, but I don't mean for a week or two. I mean maybe for a long time."

There was a long silence while Josie buttered a biscuit. "I don't know what to say, doll."

"Well, say something. I'm asking for your advice."

"What will you do for money? Where will you live? You did so well as a nanny. I still don't understand why you left that job. They paid your health benefits, and that's the thing I worry about the most."

"I guess I thought I might crash here for a while. Just until I get my bearings."

"You know we'd love to have you, if there were a little more room. But between us and the dogs, we're already on top of each other."

Serena watched her mother's large frame negotiate the tight turning space of the kitchen as she collected a saucepan off the stove and, without asking, gave Serena a second helping of fried apples. The cubbyhole in the apartment from the old days seemed like the stage set of a culinary show compared to this. Josie picked up Serena's coffee cup and dried underneath it with a dishtowel. Her movements were as professional as those of a seasoned waitress. "I hope you're not too disappointed. If you want to be here a couple of weeks or so, we know how to adjust. And if you're short on cash, we'll scrape something together. We always do."

The Irish mutthound shambled up to Serena and thrust his head under the table, into her lap, fouling the air with his sulphurous summer breath. His muzzle was damp, maybe from the lake, possibly from drinking in the toilet. Usually Serena fed him table scraps, but she nudged him away with a jab of her knee. "Go on. Shit, Jake. You're leaving a spot on my pants. Why is this dog up my ass everywhere I go? He's got hundreds of acres to romp in and he has to spend the morning under the table with his nose in my crotch."

"Scat, Jake. Serena isn't in the mood for you." Josie grabbed him by the scruff and herded him from the kitchen.

"You had Granny living here for almost two years in the spare bedroom." Even to herself, her voice sounded childish and petulant.

Josie looked over her bifocals, her no-bullshit stare. "That was different. She needed someone to care for her." Her face softened. "The selfish part of me would love to have you here. Don't you know that, darling? But you really belong in New York. That's where your friends are. That's where your life is. Also, it makes me feel safer knowing that you and Kelsey are up there together. I never liked the idea of her living in Hell's Kitchen, but at least the two of you can look out for each other. I know things aren't perfect where you are, but coming back here is not going to make everything better."

"I need a change of scenery."

"I understand, honey. But you've forgotten how you used to feel when you lived here. There were always blue periods. It seems different because you only got off the plane yesterday, and everything is fresh. Your friends are in Manhattan. Skip is there."

"Skip is on tour again. I haven't even seen him for six weeks. I told him on the phone that I was going on a retreat, and he didn't try to talk me out of it. He knows it's over. I tried travelling with him one time, but I ended up in the hotel room, watching soap operas. As for the others, those are not my friends, they're Kelsey's, and I'm nothing but a hanger-on. I'm not an actress. I call production with a headset on. I could do that job at the Burger King in Nicholasville, and get paid more for it."

"That may be what you end up doing."

"I actually have turned up something better than that. Stefano Ravel, you remember him, he's opened a child-care center, and he said they would try me out part time, just to start.

And Deeann in Lexington needs a housemate. I'm going over tomorrow to see her about it. I made some calls before I came here."

"I'm glad to hear that. But if you're asking for my benediction, you're not going to get it." She was in the sunroom now, plucking dead leaves from the spider plant and shoving them into the pocket of her housedress. "I don't want it to be said down the road that I played a part. You'll do as you please, and all I can do is tell you what I believe to be in your best interest."

Serena hadn't wanted to play her trump card, but there was no avoiding it. "I want to be closer to Dad, now that he has cancer."

Her mother had pulled a plastic bottle from the other pocket of the housecoat, and was spritzing the plants, sending a mist over them. "We're getting along fine on our own. Your father won't even let me do for him half of what I ought to. He insists on getting out there in the back yard and pruning the trees. All that's lacking is for him to end up on crutches."

"That's why he needs the two of us to gang up on him. I won't be here every day, if I'm not staying with you, but I can come over and drive him to his doctor appointments, once I get a used car. He has no business driving around so much, the way his leg is. And you don't drive."

"No, I don't." Though she had worked her way to the far end of the sun room with her spritzer, she didn't turn around. Watching her from behind, her back ever so slightly hunched, neck rigid, Serena knew what she was going to say. Josie sighed. "I guess it's settled, then. I only hope you're making the right decision."

Serena was trying without success to light another cigarette. "It's going to work out. I'll be independent and settle into my own groove. You'll see. I'm not going to be a burden to anybody. Are there more biscuits?"

" You look great."

"Do I? I feel kind of fat. These are my fat pants."

"No, are you kidding? I wish I could still get into some of those. What are they, tens? Hospital cafeteria food has been my undoing. And when I get off my shift, I want to eat everything in the house. Your hair looks cute bobbed like that. A little bit punkish, but not too. Remember when you and Kelsey both had hair down to your butts? How many guys must have pulled their pud over that."

"Yeah, remember Mr. Arden from theater class? He propositioned both of us. But at least it was on different days. Kelsey scorched him to the ground. By the time she got done lecturing him, he thought he'd been directing a morality play. Being the big sis, I settled on a different, more mature approach."

"What? You froze him out?"

"No, I went to bed with him. He couldn't get it up for some reason. I took it personally. I thought it was because my boobs weren't big enough."

She and Deeann both laughed. "God, Serena, I'm so glad you're staying here. It's going to be one big slumber party. I can't tell you how relieved I was when that housemate of mine moved out, even if I did have to pick up her part of this month's rent. Come on, let me show you your room. It's the bigger of the two, but it doesn't have a window unit. If you set the big floor fan here in the doorway, you'll get plenty of cool air from my room. Sorry about the mess. I'm not much of a housekeeper." Serena didn't know what mess she was referring to. Though the house was old, with glass knobs on the doors, worn tile in the bathroom, and big funky blinds on the windows, no clutter could be found on any of the tables, no stains or balls of lint marred the carpeting, and every object seemed to have a rack, container, or hamper. "You'll have plenty of privacy, because I've been working a lot of double shifts at the coronary care unit lately."

"How do you get psyched up? I could never do that kind of work. You have to be so super responsible."

"Sure you could do it. I flip on a switch when I go to my job, and flip it off when I leave."

"I don't know. I like lifeguarding, but then again I never had to pull anybody out of the water. The only person I ever rescued was the Annie doll. Every hour, they'd clear the pool for five minutes, to make sure nobody was floating face down in the water. That was my worst fear, that they'd find somebody I had missed."

"I'm just glad I'm not a doctor, and don't have to be on call. Sometimes on my day off, all I want to do is get a facial during the day, and hit the bars in the evening. You wouldn't believe the pressure."

"Deeann, about the rent—I'm flat broke right now, but I'm going to start work this week."

"Don't worry about it. I can float us until you get your first paycheck. Right now, the important thing is for you to get settled in. You want some coffee?" Deeann stuck a filter in the Melita and set a scrubbed, gleaming teapot on the stove. After school, she enrolled right away in a diploma program, and by twenty, she was already a nurse. From what she'd told Serena, she had a lot of responsibility and seniority on her intensive care unit, and sometimes went out on emergency transport calls in a helicopter to outlying areas. As soon as she got home she turned into a party girl. No doubt she could have bought a house already, the way she was always willing to work night shifts and extra shifts. She preferred to spend her money on extravagant outfits, ski trips to Colorado, and an occasional drive to Atlanta to see Chippendales. The crowd of young nurses she worked with revelled in going out as a gang and daring each other to stuff dollar bills into the g-string of some gyrating hunk.

Deeann had always made the most of her pleasant but not especially stunning looks. She had learned everything there was to know about the arts of makeup and fashion, and didn't flinch at spending a hundred dollars to have her hair styled or buying a pair of expensive shoes to attend a barbecue. Her sense of smell was keen, and she spent a lot of time searching in stores for perfumes, sachets, and potpourri. Though she had dated lots of men, including a number of the residents who did rotations on her floor, none of them satisfied her for very long. Most always the first comment she made about a man she'd started dating was the make of car he drove. Men without sporty cars didn't get a second chance, and even those who did were expected to spend money on her. She was astounded to discover that women sometimes paid their own way. Also, she spent a lot of time analyzing what she called, with a wild laugh, "the cuteness factor," and almost every man, sooner or later, fell short, on account of his nose or the texture of his skin, or the number of fillings she could count in his mouth when he laughed. And she was perenially surprised that the few men who did make the first cut turned out to be "such jerks." Often she talked about settling down and having kids, but it frustrated her to no end that all the cute guys with sporty cars and giving personalities appeared to have been snatched up already.

Considering how different they were, Serena wasn't quite sure how they'd stayed friends over the years. But Deeann held fast to their shared experience in children's theater, when they had played roles together in *The Children of Terezin* and *Peter Pan*. She actively pursued the friendship and didn't let Serena stay out of touch for very long. As the hot water trickled through the Melita, Deeann put her face over the cone and took a whiff of the steam.

Once she had served Serena, she pulled her chair close to the table, as if about to disclose a confidence. "Oh, Serena, it's fabulous to have you here." There was something about her tone of voice such that no matter who she was talking to, she always made that person feel they were the absolute center of her attention. If she asked you to pass the sugar, you felt that you had been let in on a cherished secret. "You look so incredible. I mean it. You have such a glow, if I didn't know better I'd ask if you were expecting. And those earrings you always turn up, from an Ethiopian street vendor or whatever, they make you look like a gypsy. The New York life obviously suits you. I don't know why you came back to this hick burg."

"Manhattan is exciting, but it wears on you after a while."

"I just admire you so much for going up there to chase your dreams. I never could have done it myself. After I played Tinkerbell, I had fantasies about becoming an actress, and I loved taking tap. Every time I get a postcard from you, I'm envious. But at least I'm realistic enough to know my limitations. I knew I couldn't tough it out subletting somebody's closet and hustling tables for money. If I want to treat myself to a hat, I want to go out and buy it and not think about whether or not I can afford it. If I ever do get married, I can assure you that the hubby and I will keep separate accounts. I'm not going to go running to him for pin money every other day." She let out another wild laugh. "I keep telling myself I'm going to get out of nursing and go do a degree in something, painting or set design. But once you've got seniority, the money's too good to give it up. They've got me where they want me."

"Don't worry. You haven't missed anything. Kelsey has fifty times the talent of you and me put together, and she's been knocking around for years doing free gigs, and now she spends half her time helping her boyfriend raise money so he can put on his plays in a church basement or a coffeehouse. I always tell her that if she had big tits and blue eyes, and threw away ninety percent of her acting ability, she'd do just fine."

"God, isn't that the truth. I thought about having breast implants. You can't believe how many of the girls from high school have gotten them. Marcia, Leslie, Beth. Lots. But you should be proud of me. Even I draw the line at that. I'm a 36C, which should be plenty for anybody. If it's that important to a guy, then he was weaned too early."

"What about Amy? I know the two of you used to be pretty tight, and I always wondered about her. Her body seemed too good to be real."

"Oh, no, those were definitely real behind the decolletage at the prom court. We had gym class together. But didn't you hear about her?"

"Hear what?"

"She killed herself."

Serena's coffee scalded the back of her throat. "Amy? But—she was going to be a veterinarian. She was good with animals." Her voice shook with outrage.

"You seem really upset. Your hand is trembling. Did you know her well?"

"No, we were acquaintances. In orchestra together. She used to jump horses at her parents' place down on Parkers Mill Road. Where are my cigarettes?"

"Right on the table in front of you. I really don't understand how anybody could, you know, do that. Can you? The thought of it gives me the willies. But maybe she was just a weak person."

"Being weak doesn't have anything to do with it."

"Don't get your dander up, hon. You'd think I was talking about you, the way you're reacting. Listen, let's talk about something else anyway. This topic is such a downer. I hadn't thought about it in ages until just now. Hey, did I tell you I'm dating one of the new residents? He drives a Celica with a sun roof. He's kind of cocky, but really a nice guy. I only wish he'd change the part in his hair."

Matt was driving the same car he'd always driven, an orange Chevy with a vinyl top that had belonged to his parents but which, in the course of his driving it so much, had at some point become his through a sort of common-law arrangement. His parents disapproved of his lifestyle, but kept up the insurance payments.

They'd had him, their only child, late in life, and treated him with the combination of indulgence and disregard one might expect of grandparents. Sometimes when Serena used to go over in the evening to their tiny frame house with the siding, behind St. Joe's Hospital, they were getting ready for a square dance. During the day, Matt's father, who sported a crew cut, worked at the GE light bulb plant. After work he changed into a white T-shirt and white painter's pants, so that he could watch television in maximum comfort. Matt's mother ran errands, sorted coupons, collected commemorative plates that she hung on the walls, and did macrame. But on certain nights of the week, the couple was transformed, the father in a western shirt with lassos and curlicues stitched across the chest, tooled boots with pointy toes and a starched bandana as red as a train robber's tied about his neck. The mother's hair would be dyed an extra shade of black, and her skirts, stiff as canvas, were heavy with rhinestones, studs, and needlepoint. On those nights the two of them moved about the house like opera stars at a dress rehearsal, Desdemona and Othello, calling to one another across the rooms for eyeliner and shoe polish. The first time she saw them, Serena decided that was the kind of marriage she wanted to have thirty years hence.

Matt, with his chubby body and standard-issue T-shirts, looked pretty much the same as always except for his coiffeur and facial hair. The last time, it had been a sensitive Jesus look, with locks past the shoulders and a tapering beard. When this was combined with his mellow FM-deejay voice singing to the accompaniment of his twelve-string guitar, she could imagine the seventeen-year-olds swooning. At least she herself had felt that way when she first met him, when he'd gone around visiting classes at the high school, the local troubador, sitting crosslegged on top of the teacher's desk, picking and strumming "Killing Me Softly" in a high tenor that often glided into a falsetto. *Telling my whole life with his words, killing me softly.* Now, when he played the occasional weekend gig at the Jefferson Davis Inn, he could easily have put the make on most any woman in the place, especially the ones who'd gotten in with fake IDs.

But he never tried. Nothing had ever happened between him and Serena, not even a glimmer of attraction on his part that she could detect. Maybe that's why she and he had been able to maintain their friendship. He had been involved, if you could call it that, with his girlfriend Shar since high school, and the two of them had lived together, off and on, since she couldn't remember when. But you could hardly call that a relationship. He and Shar, as far as that went, were like two characters in a Beckett play, Flimm and Flamm, or however they were called, so that a person couldn't rightly say whether they were husband and wife, brother and sister, mother and son, or even which was which.

This time, he'd cut his hair almost as short as his father's, and had grown a Fu Manchu and long sideburns to go with it. Serena had always chided him that he was trying to compete with Eric Clapton. But there was comfort in knowing he would show up with a new face in the identical burnt-orange car each time she came to town, the vinyl top a little worse for the wear but the motor still running.

"You playing many gigs this summer?"

"Not that much. Me and a couple of guys are trying to get together a demo tape so we can drive down to Nashville and shop it around. Did I tell you I've been writing country music? It's a whole new groove for me."

"Weren't you working on that demo tape last time I was here?"

"Yeah, well, that was with a different band. We broke up because one of the guys got a job framing houses. He said he was sick of selling plasma. We'd been over to the donor place so many times the woman who draws blood would wave us away through the plate glass window when she saw us coming. When we went in anyway, she told us we needed to eat more kale and not drop by so much. She said that the Piggly Wiggly was having a sale on spinach and kale, and gave us five dollars out of her handbag. But this band I'm with now is more serious. One of them is friends with a guy who has set up a recording studio in his basement. He's got all the equipment, and is willing to give us a discount on cutting a demo. The only hitch is that he's a fanatic about the wall of sound thing. I just don't think that the wall of sound goes too well with country music."

"I'm glad to hear that you're working on something new. Where's Shar? I thought she might come along tonight. You all still together?"

"Ah, you know. We're living above the leather shop over in Chevy Chase. She said she had to work late there today. She's had a lot of orders for the painted leather earrings. I keep telling her she ought to go solo and sell them at the crafts fairs, instead of working for an hourly wage and letting the owners have all the profit. But she isn't a real entrepreneur type."

"Whenever I'm in town, it seems like Shar is busy. Last time she wouldn't go along to breakfast because she had an ingrown toenail. I always get the feeling she doesn't care much for me."

"Really? I thought I was the only one she treated that way."

"No, I'm serious. She acts paranoid. It seems worse every time I see her, which is usually through a crack in the door. Maybe she thinks I'm giving her competition. She's been nursing that notion for ten or twelve years now. Just once, I'd like to sit down face to face with her and explain that she doesn't have anything to worry about."

"I don't think you should tell her that."

"Why not?"

"I mean, well, sure, it's already obvious. Like you said. Anyway, if you said that to her, it would only put an idea in her mind."

"So she is paranoid."

"She dwells on things a lot." He gave her a sly smile. "Besides, just because you're paranoid doesn't mean they're not out to get you. Hey, did you hear Robbie was working as a river guide?"

"God, I haven't thought about him in a long time. We stopped writing. So he doesn't still live here?"

"He comes back for part of the year. Always brown as a nut. I haven't seen him in a few months, but he'll be blowing in next week at the latest, because business drops off on the Colorado when the canyon gets too hot."

"Remember how the three of us, you, me, and him, used to snuggle down under army blankets at night and eat tortilla chips when we trekked up in the summer to Dagmar's place on Lake Michigan?"

"Yeah, but what I remember better is the time that Robbie and I had bought ten hits of blotter and decided to do them all at once.

We were going to sleep in that little screened-in fort on stilts in Dagmar's backyard, at the edge of the woods, and me and Robbie ran an extension cord out there so we could hook up an old record player that we found in her basement. We got in the fort, and the acid literally knocked us down. It hit us so hard we just crouched on the floor and hugged each other like death for hours. There was a lot of wind stirring the trees up, and we thought the branches were trying to tear the roof away so they could reach in and get us. We bawled our heads off. The phonograph record, a live album by The Kinks, kept replaying, over and over again, and scaring the shit out of us even worse, but both of us were too paralyzed to go over five feet and turn off the record, so we listened to it all night, soaked in sweat and pissing our pants. Every so often the emcee would say 'Ladies and gentlemen, The Kinks,' and then this horrible hooting and roaring and stomping started, like they were bringing out the victim for a human sacrifice, and then after the music smashed along for an eternity, babe, you really got me going, you got me so I don't know what I'm doing, you really got me, you really got me, you really got me, you really got me, then at last there was silence, and we thought we would be okay, but then the emcee would say again in that same diabolical voice, 'Ladies and gentlemen, The *Kiiinks*!' and it would start all over. Finally, Robbie and I started coming down, enough that I was able to stand up, lurch over and turn off the record player, and I'll never forget, Robbie looked at me, you could see in his eyes that he was grateful, the wind had died down and it had gotten real still and quiet, and he said in a whisper, 'Now I know what they mean by coming out of the kinks.' And we just laid down on the floor and howled."

"We were pretty fucked up in those days, weren't we?"

"Yeah, we were pretty fucked up."

"Where are we going tonight?"

"High on Rose, so you can have some of those good greasy enchiladas you like so much. Or let's stop by the leather shop so you can see Shar, then when she gets off maybe we can all eat at the apartment."

"You don't have to do that. I don't want to make problems for you. I only wondered how she was getting along."

"No, I'll pick up some fajita fixings and we can make dinner. Shar will be glad you're back."

The leather shop had a strong, definite, pleasant scent that enveloped her as she walked through the door. A bell tinkled. Tooled belts and hats hung from pegs on the wall. Purses were suspended overhead, as in a bazaar. She could fairly hear their straps creak in the breeze of the oscillating fan. In the midst of exquisite goods emanating their single dark perfume, Serena almost forgot why she had come.

Then she caught sight of Shar behind the glass counter, peering at her like an animal trapped unexpectedly in its burrow. Shar had always had salient eyes, and they never looked more so than now against the flat plane of her face, half hidden beneath her bangs. Her expression seldom changed. She wore the same outfit of tights, heavy pleated skirt and shapeless blouse that she'd favored when she worked behind the counter of Volunteers, the Salvation-Army-type store her father owned. Apparently she chose her wardrobe from the store's own second-hand stock, selecting the garments that had been picked over and left behind even by people who were looking for necessary bargains. It was hard to think of Shar serving the public, because nothing whatsoever about Shar's demeanor suggested that she had any desire to wait on people. Her presence in the leather shop, as it had in the thrift shop, bereaved it of the enticing sense of a find about to be discovered, and made the place seem more like an archive for specialists where few visited, and even fewer were granted entry.

"Hi, Shar."

"Serena."

"I'm living back in Lexington now, over in Chevy Chase, and I thought I'd drop by to say hello and let you know I'm around."

"What a surprise."

"Matt tells me you're making and selling leather earrings. I'd love to see some. I've sort of made a reputation for myself as the earring queen, and I'm always on the lookout for new ones."

"You don't say. The queen." Shar motioned to the right end of the counter with her head. The rest of her remained immobile and immutable beneath folds of clothing. Under the glass countertop, the leather had been crinkled so that each earring made the shape of a fan or seashell, handpainted with miniature designs.

"They're gorgeous. You did these? I mean, I'm not surprised, I remember the ceramics you used to make in pottery class. I just didn't know you'd branched out into earrings too. I'll take, let's see, those right there, and those other squiggly ones. How much are they?"

"You can have them."

"No, no. I want to support an up and coming artisan."

Shar shrugged. "Whatever. They're twelve dollars a pair."

"You really ought to consider going into business for yourself. I've been to I don't know how many craft fairs, and I never see anything this nice."

Shar gave Matt a hooded look, her lids sliding down over the balls of her eyes. "With my and Matt's combined salaries, I don't think we'd qualify for a small business loan. At least here I can get as many hours as I want, and keep money coming in until Matt wins the country music entertainer of the year award. Only I don't know where we'll put the trophy. We don't have any bookshelves. We still own one of those tables that used to be a cable spool, and we found our couch by driving around in alleys on a sunny day, so there'd be less chance of varmints breeding in the stuffing."

Matt blushed easily, and his face had turned almost salmon. "Serena came over to have dinner with us. I thought I'd surprise you."

"If she can find anything up there in the refrigerator, she's welcome to it. By the way, the freezer needs to be defrosted again. The door won't shut. Since it's almost empty, you might as well turn it off and set a bucket underneath. Don't use a sharp knife like last time, so you don't puncture the tubes again and let all the Freon out."

"Okay, I'll do it. But first I'm going to make some beef fajitas. Doesn't that sound good? We stopped and bought the ingredients. They had sirloin marked down that was about to expire in the meat section."

"You all go ahead. I'm not supposed to close up shop for another hour."

"Come on, honey. It's a dead night. Nobody ever comes in here on Wednesday evenings. Close up early. Who will know?"

"I'll see what I do. " She busied herself impaling receipts on a spindle.

Serena and Matt climbed the stairwell in the narrow space between two buildings. The numbers of the address had fallen off the facade, except for the number 1/2. There was no doorknob on the outside of the door. Matt pulled a pair of pliers from the mailbox and turned the scarred spindle. When they entered the kitchen, Matt took a knife and a cutting board from one of the drawers, and set it on the counter. "Here, slice this thin for me, then I'll marinate it for a few minutes in some beer. I'll get the hibachi going."

Serena yanked the meat from the sack, tore it loose from the white butcher's paper, and savaged it with the knife.

"Whoa, there, hoss. This isn't Benihana. Take your time."

"Why does she act so shitty to me? I've never said an unkind word to her in my life. Is it because of my looks? I can't help the way I was born. It's not like I'm flirtatious."

"It's not you. It doesn't have anything to do with you."

"Well, what about you? Why do you let her talk to you that way? Try cutting her sarcasm with this knife, and see how deep you go."

"She's been through a lot."

"So she's been through a lot. I've been through a few things myself. And I'm sure you have too. You don't have to make excuses for her. The truth is, she's always been that way.

Besides, no matter what she's been through, that attitude of hers can only make her situation worse. She'll never get over whatever is eating at her. How can anybody help her when she repulses every attempt to be friendly?"

"Forget about it. It's not worth spoiling your visit over. Here, let me cut the sirloin, and you fill the bong on the mantlepiece. There are matches in the tin beside it." Matt sliced the sirloin in thin strips in spite of the knife's dull edge. He tossed the strips into a bowl of beer as if feeding bait to fish. She did as he said, took a toke off the bong, and held it for him while he did the same. "Some people are never happy, their whole lives," he said, "and nothing you do will make them that way." He held the smoke in as he talked in a raspy voice, the way an adolescent might. His face had a mischievous smile on it. His pleasure in the ritual of smoking hadn't changed in the least. It made her want to reach out and stroke his cheek. Matt gave her the same kind of comfort she got from having a cat in her lap. Everywhere she'd lived, with a man or alone, she'd always made sure she had a cat. There had always been the acid smell of the litterbox to contend with, but it was worth it.

"If you can't make her happy, then why do you stay?"

"Because I feel a sense of obligation. We've broken off two or three times, and I've moved out, but I always end up coming back."

"What kind of obligation?"

"Never mind. She's had her share." He wiped his hands clean on a dishtowel and put on a record. The needle dropped. Merle Haggard's voice let fly a litany of melodic, misogynistic, husky complaints, his voice permanently ruined by whisky.

"I didn't know you listened to Merle Haggard. That's redneck music."

"I've always listened to Merle Haggard. I never fessed up to it, that's all. I kept it tucked inside the cover of my Dan Fogelberg."

"My mother is crazy about Merle Haggard too. Every time she hears 'If We Make It Through December,' she gets weepy."

"Oh, I know all about that. Last winter I drove out to Chalk Lake, and your mom and me put Merle on her old record player, dished up some mulled wine out of the crockpot, threw our arms around each other, and sang along together. There's nothing better when you're feeling sorry for yourself. It doesn't get you anywhere, but you can wallow in your misery for a while. I've always thought the phrase should be Unhappy as a pig in shit, then more people could use it."

When he'd gotten the hibachi going on the balcony by putting an open-ended tin can over the coals, he spread the avocado, cheese, onions, containers of sour cream and salsa out over the counter and went to work. She'd never thought about him as someone who cooked. But he was methodical and absorbed in the preparations, mincing and grating with a particular, almost fussy attention to texture. He even cleaned up after himself as he went. She could imagine him taking care of Shar if she had a bout of pneumonia, changing the sheets, wiping her amorphous body down with a washcloth in the middle of the night, mixing whisky and honey together in a cup, keeping Merle's music turned down low as he sat up in a far corner to keep watch over her.

After he'd placed the meat on the grill, he took out his guitar, fitted the capo across the steel strings, and picked a couple of his new countryesque compositions for her. Long ago she had learned that the quickest way to ensure Matt wouldn't play for her was to ask him to play. He was perversely, almost willfully shy about it. The spirit had to move him, Quakerlike, before he would perform in private, and though he professed to be rehearsing all the time with one band or another, he seldom sought out new gigs. She couldn't help noticing how accomplished his technique had become. She, who was supposed to have such a good ear and an intuitive feel for the violin, had given it up easily, while Matt, who spent God knows how many of his waking hours hammering at the frets, continued to languish in making his way in the world as a performer. But every time she heard him he'd improved, and now he sounded professional. As much affection as Serena felt for Matt, she had always considered him stationary, static, adrift, coasting toward a dead end, when in fact she could see that there was something quite purposeful about him. He'd never stopped reading Buddhist philosophy, whereas for the rest of their group it had only been a predictable phase. He'd never sold any of his songs, or made any money to speak of off his musical performances, but it remained true that he was always "working on" his music. The vagueness of that phrase had deceived her into believing he was rehashing the same half-dozen songs year after year. During her last visit, though, she'd discovered that he'd written upwards of two hundred compositions. He forever talked about going to Nashville or L.A., but part of him seemed to consider that once he'd written a song, it had served its purpose.

"That's beautiful. It kind of puts me in mind of 'Girl From the North Country.' Do you ever think about what you'll do with the songs of yours that remain unpublished when you die?"

He switched in mid-tune from the song he was playing to another that kept alternating keys. Apparently he was composing a new song as they talked. Matt never uttered any romantic cliches about inspiration or needing to be cloistered with his guitar. "I don't know. Maybe Roy Acuff will buy them all for fifty bucks."

"No, I mean it. What will become of them? Doesn't that concern you?"

"You can have them if you want."

"Stop teasing."

"I'm not. Nobody else has asked me for them, so if you want them, they're yours. I'll have a living will made up next week. I can get one for free at Legal Services. I've been meaning to stop over there, but I have so few possessions it hardly seemed worth it."

"You're assuming that I'm going to outlive you."

Matt stopped playing and gave her an uncharacteristic hard look. "Don't say stuff like that. Not even if you're joking."

"Well, neither of us knows who will survive the other. That's the truth."

"I don't care. I don't like people close to me to talk about themselves that way." He tried to pick back up the tune he'd been working out, but he'd lost the thread of his composition. He laid down the guitar. "Shit. Those fajitas have probably burned up. I can smell them from here." When he fished them off the grill, only three of the strips had charred completely, but he threw out all the ones even slightly in doubt. "Here. I think this one turned out okay."

"Aren't we going to wait for Shar?"

"She's not coming. She probably walked over to Two Keys for a drink."

There were no chairs, and the couch had a severe dip in the middle, so they ate sitting cross-legged on the floor. The fajitas, spicy, succulent, aromatic, tasted good, but Matt only nibbled at his food. When she had finished, she laid her plate on the carpet, walked over to him on her knees, and laid her head up against his chest. "You don't mind, do you?"

"No, of course not." He put his woolly arms around her.

"That's nice. Nobody's been touching me much lately." She moved her head to and fro gently, like someone trying to catch the air from a fan. The feel of his Fu Manchu against her cheek gave her pleasure. When she turned her face toward him to look at his mustache, he kissed her on the lips. She started back, breaking the loose hold of his arms. He didn't try to detain her. "I'm sorry," she said, trying to pretend it hadn't startled her as much as it had. "I just wasn't expecting it."

"No problem." He had already stumbled to his feet. His body, bearlike, unbalanced, stooped to clear the plates from the floor.

Serena followed him into the kitchen. "Believe me, I wouldn't mind. And I'd rather it be with a friend, somebody I care about, than picking somebody up in a bar. But with Shar downstairs, it doesn't seem too smart."

His shoulders gave an involuntary shrug. "She's not down there. She won't come back until she thinks you're gone. She's going to assume we went to bed together whether we do or not.

Maybe that's why I kissed you, to at least get something for my trouble. That's why she didn't come up, because if she stayed here with us it wouldn't be hypothetically possible for us to have done anything, and so she couldn't accuse me. You're right, though. I shouldn't even be thinking about stuff like that."

"You understand, don't you, Matt? I don't want any more ill will between Shar and me than exists already."

Matt set the dirty plates in the sink and reached inside the frost-encrusted freezer to find the dial. He groped, frowning, like someone who has hidden his life savings in a clever place only to find it's been stolen. When he extracted his arm, it was covered with crystalline flakes of ice. "It's been a long time since she and I made love. Not that we ever did a lot, but it's nice once in a while to remember that you still exist from the neck down." He sighed. "They found a big malignant cyst on Shar's ovary a few months ago. Supposedly it hadn't metastasized, but they removed them to be safe, and did the whole hysterectomy thing. They say they think they got everything, but she'll have to keep being screened every six months. Before, she never even mentioned having kids, but of course now that she can't, she wants one. Not that she'd be able to conceive even if it were medically possible, because you still have to have intercourse with somebody first. She won't even let me get near her. She says she doesn't feel like a woman anymore. I don't want to be unfaithful to her, but you know, I'm only in my thirties, and sometimes I do have the urge. If something doesn't happen soon, I mean if there isn't some kind of break in this standoff, I may have to move out again."

"I didn't have any idea. I'm sorry I criticized her. You're right to stay with her. I used to think sex was everything, and I was such a hot tamale that if I went even a few days without, I felt it. But now it doesn't seem such a big deal. Other things are more important. Like I said, I'm starved right now, but to tell you the truth, it's been weeks since I even thought about it. What's happening to all of us? We're not even to middle age, and it seems like everybody I talk to these days is or knows somebody who is either sick or ailing or dying or dead. Our life spans are going back to what they were in the Middle Ages. I feel like I've crossed over an invisible threshold, one I didn't even know was there, and I'll never be able to cross back again. It spooks the hell out of me."

"Serena, I've been thinking about an idea for a while now. I've been reading the real estate classifieds, and you can buy a farm with like a hundred or more acres on it for not that much money. Everybody is so hard up that farms are going for nothing, especially those ones down by the Kentucky River where the land slopes so much, you could stand on the road, drop a bowling ball and watch it roll across the acreage and down to the river, picking up speed the whole way. With so many foreclosures, farmers would rather sell for a loss than have to take bankruptcy. We're talking a hundred fifty thousand dollars max, for a huge spread of land, the farmhouse, barns, the whole deal. I don't have any way of knowing if or when Shar's problem is going to come back. I want her, us, to have something now, before our lives get completely used up. She's already given up on hers, but I'm hoping I can bring her back from the dead, so to speak."

"That's an incredible idea. A farm. Still, a hundred fifty thousand dollars. And where are you going to get the down payment?"

"First off, I know Shar has a few thousand socked away from her grandparents. She's saving it for her funeral expenses, because now that she has a pre-existing condition, we can't get life insurance. I haven't said anything to her yet, but I'm almost sure I can talk her into putting that up as a down payment. Since it's equity, she won't lose it. And now that you're back, you could go in with us if you wanted. Robbie, too. Once he returns from his river gig, I'm going to lay the proposal out for him. The four of us are finally all back here together, and nobody has any other real obligations, so what better time?"

"I don't have any savings. I'd be willing to bet Robbie doesn't either."

"It doesn't matter. If you two can find a job, we'll pool our paychecks and cover the mortgage payments with plenty to spare. It won't be much more than we're all spending on rent collectively right now. We'll find a farm close enough that we can commute to Lexington to our jobs. And you know what? I've been talking to a guy at one of the horse farms who wants to take me on as an apprentice blacksmith. I met him at the track, and he was making huge bets, I'm talking in the thousands. He says blacksmiths who work for the thoroughbred farms and tracks make big bucks. I'll only be earning five dollars an hour to start, but once I'm on my own, there's no telling how much I can pull in. If everybody pitches in, we shouldn't have any problems."

"But what would we raise? You don't know anything about farming."

"That's the beauty. We leave it in its pristine state. Animals could roam around, deer, rabbits, or whatever, and the trees and wildflowers can take over if they want. We cultivate the amount we want for our personal needs, and let nature take its course with the rest."

"I barely just got here, so I'm not sure I could commit to something like that. Also, I'm not too sanguine about me and Shar living under the same roof."

"Come on. I thought you were the free spirit. It will work out. We'll make it work. Once she gets out in the country, her whole disposition will change, I guarantee it. And don't you remember how you always used to talk about moving out to the country, raising a huge herb and flower garden? So when are you going to act on that urge? Isn't that why you moved back from Manhattan, to get away from all the urban stress? Tell me that's not true. Goin' where the water tastes like wine, gonna jump in the water, stay drunk all the time." He sang to her in his most persuasive falsetto, dancing around her.

She laughed. "Get away. You still can't dance. I've never seen you so fired up about anything before. You sound like an ecological real estate agent. I didn't know you had it in you. Okay, I have been getting pretty jangled. But I haven't even started work here yet. I'll tell you what. I'll think about it, as a possibility down the road."

"Fair enough. Remember, though, that the interest rates could jump back up at any time. Will you help me sell Robbie on the idea when he gets here? There has to be at least four of us to swing it. Everything will be like old times, only better. Nobody's going to call us deadheads or burnouts. I'm sick of everybody looking at me and thinking Yeah, there goes another casualty of the seventies."

When they entered High on Rose, Robbie had already staked out a table in the far corner, and was motioning to them. He stood up to sidle around the table and give her a hug. His wild black hair, shoulder length, had sun-bleached enough to bring out the reddish tones, and his skin was burned a deep, lasting brown. Robbie had always been rangy, but the combination of his thinness and his overbite, combined with his earnest scientific bent, used to give him a faintly goofy expression. Now the overbite accentuated the fullness of his lips. His features remained delicate, almost effeminate, and his body had taken on a more solid, masculine look. He wore a headband and a sleeveless muscle shirt. His arms went on forever as they wrapped around her. She came chest-high on him and he smelled like soap.

"You look good. You're—well, I don't know how to put it politely. You're not as geeky as you used to be."

"I'll consider that a compliment. You're in good shape yourself. You've stayed fit. Looks like you've kept up with your swimming." He and Matt had already locked in a bone-jarring embrace, moving stiff-legged in a slow circle, like wrestlers on a dance floor. There had always existed between the two of them an easy physical rapport. They were forever touching and squeezing and looping their arms about each other's necks as they talked, their mouths inches apart. They didn't care what people thought, and sometimes they exaggerated in public just to provoke customers at nearby tables.

"Come on, you guys. Cut the male bonding."

"Male bondage, you mean."

"Whatever. Let's sit down. I'm thirsty."

"The wench is peevish."

"Verily, she maketh her displeasure known."

The waitress came over. "What'll you have?"

Serena took in the bottles behind the bar at a glance. "I don't know. I'm not in the mood for beer, really. I think I'll have a white Russian."

"A white Russian? I'm not going to be outdone by little sister's East coast savoir faire. I'll have a Manhattan. Man, what is this shit all over my shoes? I'm beginning to think they throw down sawdust in here so they won't have to sweep the floor."

Matt looked disgruntled. "This isn't a fern bar. I thought we were going to share a pitcher. A draft for me."

"So you've been working as a river guide." She was keenly aware of the hum of customers at nearby tables. Everyone in the room sounded animated, antic, as they disgorged privileged information in a cacophony of competing conversations. As a waitress, she had always been surprised at how frank people's speech could get in a public place. Even now, she could hear a man complaining about his herpes at the next table over, how it went from dormant to active at the most inopportune times. She wasn't listening as attentively as she should to Robbie's recitation of his spring and summer on the Colorado, but the beauty of his talking head with its shining locks made her tune into him.

"—and it's mostly these rich executives who want to turn macho for a week, away from their wives and girlfriends. Not only do we guides have to load all the food in watertight containers, talk the greenhorns through the rapids, point out the natural formations and flora, build the fires, do the cooking, but on top of it we have to create the illusion for them that they're in danger, close but not too close to being swept away by the current. Otherwise, they don't feel they've gotten their money's worth. They ride you hard. And the money isn't even that good."

"Why do you stay at it, if you don't like it?"

He smiled. "Because I'm a whore, you know that, Serena. I'll do anything for filthy lucre, even in small quantities."

"Oh, right, a whore. You're about the most ethical person I know."

"Hey, don't insult Robbie. That hurts a man's pride, being called ethical."

"I like being outdoors. Naturally, the executives want to feel secure that we guides are always in control, and I can see them glancing back at me in the raft as we approach the class four rapids, to see whether I look worried or not. What I don't tell them is how many people really do drown on that river every year, not with our outfit, but the kayakers and the teenagers in canoes who want to do it solo. Some of those rapids are wicked, if you're not used to reading the river. All it takes is one bad flip of the kayak, or one wrong turn of the canoe. But when you're seventeen, nobody can talk to you about death. Intellectually, they know their life is finite, but they don't feel it in their body. I actually watched three guys, all teenagers, buy the farm, saw it with my own eyes. One second they were whooping it up, splashing each other with paddles, and the very next second they were gone. That fast. Man, my arms are sore. My last trip was an eight-day deal." As he massaged his triceps, Serena could appreciate how developed his arms had become, the muscles rippling beneath his exploring fingers.

Matt seemed anxious to change the subject. "Speaking of buying farms, what would you say if I told you that me and Shar and you and Serena could all go together and purchase a bona-fide Kentucky farm for peanuts?"

"Does that mean that me and little sister have to be a unit?" He turned to her, eyes twinkling as always, and without having to lean forward, he reached out to massage her neck with his hand. Part of what made him so appealing to people is that he never seemed worried about anything. On the contrary, he was the one whose reassuring presence made others feel less blue. He'd taken his degree in engineering, then gave up the profession after only two years, because the contractor he worked for tried to transfer him onto a defense-related project. Matt circulated the story about Robbie taking a stand at his job, but Robbie himself, modest as always, never mentioned it. When he told his employers why he was leaving, he was so affable about it that they tried to persuade him to stay on; he got along so well with all his co-workers, they could rotate him off so he'd only have to work on defense a couple of days each month, when they needed his specific expertise. He was too creative to lose, they wanted an iconoclast on the team who would keep them honest, and they offered him a pay raise to soothe his qualms. He politely, almost apologetically declined, telling them it wasn't a political statement, and went to work for an art gallery. It didn't seem to trouble him in the least to abandon the career he'd trained for.

"How can you be so happy all the time?" Serena wanted to know. "It isn't natural."

He looked even more amused. "Why do you ask me that? Do I have a shit-eating grin on my face or something?"

"You were talking a second ago about those three boys who died, and it doesn't seem to affect you."

"Sure it does. I felt really sad about it. I had to help fish the bodies out, and I tried to give CPR. But after a couple of days I didn't think that much about it. It's not like I knew them. If it had been you or Matt, sure, I'd have to get over that, and it would take me longer."

"But you could."

"Could what?"

"Get over the death of me or Matt. I'm just curious."

He took a sip of his Manhattan, and made a face. "Whew. I'm definitely not a highball man. It would be hard, but I'd have to. Life is for the living. I only get one life myself, so I can't spend it mourning. If I'd been the one to drown, I wouldn't want you all to spend the rest of your lives beating your breasts over it."

"I don't think I could ever get over it if something happened to either one of you."

"Whoa. I'm not going to touch that one. What about you, Matt? Would you miss us if we were gone?"

"I don't want to talk about this morbid shit. I need to order another beer."

"I'm buying this round," said Robbie. "Listen, I think your farm idea is cool. Only problem is, I'm impecunious. With seasonal work, it's almost like room and board and a gratuity. All you do is cover your expenses."

"What about your engineering degree? There are all kinds of civil projects around here, you know, boring stuff like re-designing sewer systems or whatever. You could make a good salary. See, the idea is we get a big tract of land out in the country, and don't even cultivate it, unless we wanted to raise ourselves a little homegrown stash back in the weeds somewhere. Let the game run free."

Robbie laughed. "I see you've planned my future for me in my absence, buddy. It's a crazy notion. Then again, when somebody gets a wild hair, I'm usually right there behind them. I never let my work interfere with my lifestyle. But if me working as an engineer means I can help the four of us have our own private little commune, with trees on it, to hike around on, maybe hunt with a crossbow, stock the pond with some crappie, I could get into that. Let's keep talking about it."

"I'm going to let you and Serena talk about it while I go take a whizz. Order me another Mic, okay?" He navigated among the tightly grouped tables, moving his hips with a well-practiced toreador sway to keep from striking against any of them.

"That Matt, man, he's always plotting. Still waters. Usually, though, it has something to do with Muscle Shoals or the Grand Ole Opry. I doubt he'll go through with it, but it's fun to fantasize."

"Don't be so sure," she said, eating the cherry out of his Manhattan. "He wants to do it for Shar. You'd be surprised at what people will rise to when they're really attached to somebody. It brings out unsuspected sides of their personalities. And Robbie, I want to ask you one favor."

"What's that?"

"Don't call me 'little sister.'"

"Why not? I've always called you that. You never seemed to mind it before."

"Because I'm not your little sister."

She asked Robbie to drive her home. Matt wanted the three of them to bar-hop over to the Jefferson Davis Inn, there was a swing band there called the Saddle Bangers, and he could get them in without a cover, he knew the people, they'd be waved through if they came with him. Without saying anything, Serena made it clear that she wasn't in the mood. She knew Matt was trying to avoid going home to Shar, and he'd probably stay out regardless, but she didn't want to fill the role of the homewrecker in Shar's mind. Robbie, eager not to displease either of them, said he would try to meet Matt there later. He drove Serena around for a while, seeming to sense that she didn't want to be taken home right away. Perhaps he thought that she had something important on her mind, but she kept silent.

So they drove. Robbie kept up a stream of genial complaints about how Lexington changed every time he moved away for a few months, how new suburbs kept being added to the city, which now extended far beyond Man O'War. He used to be able to ride his bicycle and be wading in tall grass and countryside within fifteen minutes. That's what had made Lexington special, kept it from being a cow town. In a few years, the way developers were snapping things up, there wouldn't be any more farms to be had for love or money within a fifty-mile radius of Lexington. Maybe Matt's idea wasn't so farfetched after all. Harrodsburg Road and Parkers Mill had gotten all chopped up, there were practically no horse farms anymore either, because they'd all been subdivided too. Calumet Farm was even on the auction block, so he'd heard.

Fog lay in the bottoms, as always, but backlit now by street lamps. Black tobacco barns set on rises looked as anachronistic as feudal castles among the villages of surrounding red brick houses, spanking new. "Calumet Farm," she said almost wistfully. "I guess the horsey people can't maintain the lifestyle anymore. The closest I came to that set was helping cater the Tattersalls auction once, for three bucks an hour. And we employees took home the leftovers. I ate canapés for supper for the next two weeks."

"I didn't even have that much contact. I still like to look at the horse farms, though."

"Yeah, me too," she said, trying to be companionable. But it wasn't really true. She wanted to share in his idealized vision of the past, yet she couldn't, not tonight. It made her unaccountably restless to be confined to a car, especially one with bucket seats, where all you could do was pretty much stare through the windshield. The ergonomics of the situation had a way of forcing you to be nostalgic. Without looking at one another, you were supposed to relive and describe all the wonderful past times you had spent together, and she above all didn't want to settle into a conversational groove about the comfortable friendship they'd experienced—for instance, how he'd been the one to turn her onto marijuana.

They were supposed to laugh about it, as they always did, and she was supposed to say he had corrupted her, or else they'd remember other youthful indiscretions, like the way they used to climb over his back fence onto the golf course to retrieve lost balls among the trees to sell to the weekend golfers. One evening she reasoned that there had to be hundreds of golf balls accumulated at the bottom of the pond on the fifteenth hole, and she told him to fetch a bucket, his waterproof flashlight, and his diving mask. She had volunteered to dive to the bottom to dredge up as many golf balls as she could. She'd jumped into the pond without hesitation, in the dark. When she broke the surface with the first handful of treasure, she chucked it into the waiting bucket, her body streaked with dirt and dark as peat.

Though he'd never said so directly, it was the quality he admired most in her, in anyone, that kind of risk-taking, because he liked to take physical risks too, and sometimes demanded it of others, but for that very reason he should have known that it was no big deal, because unlike most people, she had no fear of water. Deep, shallow, murky, clear, night or day, it made no difference.

Still, he held an exaggerated respect for what he considered her bravado, the more so because she was a woman. They had shinnied up the steel cable of the elevator shaft in the nursing home behind Turfland Mall when it was still under construction. And she had always been the one to secure their booze. One of her ruses was to rush into a liquor store, alone, with keys in her hand, sobbing and muttering about a fight with an apocryphal boyfriend as she pulled a six-pack from the cooler and threw it and her money on the counter. The male clerks never called her on it, partly because they didn't want to upset her anymore than she was already, since most of them had been raised to call everybody Ma'am, and partly because most men, in her experience, were turned on by the spectacle of an anonymous jilted woman openly weeping tears of love in their presence, and they didn't want to break the spell of whatever fantasy they had going in their head by asking her for identification.

Cream ale had been her and Robbie's drink of preference. There was a storm sewer outlet, a concrete pipe several feet in diameter underneath Beacon Hill Road, that had become their safe haven. Often they would simply stash the bottles of ale in the creek's flow, beneath the jutting pipe, to keep them cool, and return that night to drink them, their bodies scrunched up as they sat inside against the curving wall. Another item she purchased was Swisher Sweets, disgusting cherry cigars that they would puff together while they sipped their ale. Once in a while, after she got a buzz on, she might crawl further into the drainage pipe to the point where it started to narrow, then further beyond. Even he didn't like that, and he would protest, feebly, but she would squeeze through anyway, and he would have to follow, until the concrete became so girdled about them that they couldn't move, their breath close and echoing, and then they'd have to back out, one excruciating inch at a time. Once in a while, after performing this strenuous exercise, they would neck, covering each other's faces and lips with kisses, but that was about it. He had never advanced beyond rubbing his hands frantically up and down her back. She couldn't decide whether it was because her breasts seemed too small to his adolescent mind to warrant closer inspection, or perhaps because he hadn't known how to undo a bra clasp and didn't want to betray his ignorance.

Their pubescent adventures seemed excruciatingly mild and predictable when she thought about them now, and she had no desire to return to them in talk. He hadn't corrupted her, nor she him, if the truth be known. She'd spent no real time with Robbie in the last few years, and whatever had occurred before didn't seem particularly relevant now. That didn't leave her with much to say, because the only other option was to have a strenuously meaningful conversation, the kind of conversation she and Matt and Robbie fell into on the long drive up to Michigan one summer, after which they all three felt secure in the knowledge that they'd plumbed each other's souls to the deepest recesses, when in fact they hadn't discovered a single thing about one another they hadn't known before.

Now she knew him less than ever, and he didn't have a clue about her. Unlike her, he seemed perfectly self-contained. He'd convinced himself that he was open to other people's inner lives, but the truth was, he didn't have the stomach for it. He didn't want to know any more about the world or other people than what came to him in the natural course of things. It was important to him that others be healthy, fit, like himself. When they used to ride the city bus downtown sometimes to do a little light shoplifting at the camping store and then buy lunch at the Woolworth's counter, it made him uncomfortable to sit close to the chronic bus riders who wore the forlorn look of the permanently ill. Once she'd caught mono, and the whole time she had it, he didn't come to visit her because he was afraid of catching it himself. Afterward, he'd tried teasing her about getting the kissing disease, wanting to know who'd given it to her, but she'd gotten very angry at him for abandoning her, and he hadn't brought up the subject again since, even when they reminisced.

Matt and Shar didn't even have much love between them, but Matt remained devoted to Shar, to the point where he had cooked up an alternative life for her. If Shar passed away before him, there was no question that he would spend the rest of his days mourning her. Serena herself still thought almost every day about Sean, her friend from junior high who had moved out to Phoenix and gotten killed at seventeen when a drunk driver off a reservation ran a red light and demolished his van. Because she hadn't been able to attend the memorial service in Arizona, she still didn't quite believe that it had happened.

She remembered how he had served as go-between in junior high for a friend of his who had a crush on her, telling her that when this friend kissed her, her toes would curl. The claim had been so preposterous that she let herself be persuaded to try. With his mass of blond curls, crooked-tooth smile, gangly body, and horn-rimmed glasses, Sean himself made for an unlikely stud, but while the rest of the pubescent boys stood around posturing and making exaggerated claims about their conquests, Sean for the most part kept silent in his own behalf and went straight for the halter top. After they'd felt each other up good, she would entertain him by saving up her breath and burping the entire alphabet in a froggy voice. Every time, he fell over laughing as though it were the first time she'd performed the trick. Hardly a day went by that she didn't still think of Sean, because she'd formed the idea that if a week passed without anybody summoning up his memory, he would be lost from the world for good, gone into some ill-defined spirit netherworld, so she kept her silent vigil.

The car coasted down the severe dip in Lane Allen Road. Robbie made a left past the drainage ditch that ran smack up the middle of Beacon Hill. The length of exposed concrete pipe hove into view, but she didn't give it more than a glance. "There's the cave of doom," said Robbie.

"Hm."

"Don't give me that monosyllabic shit. You going to tell me seeing that doesn't take you back?"

"I don't know," she answered in a melancholy voice. "I suppose it does."

"You're in a funny mood tonight, Serena." He reached over to put his arm around her, and she shrugged it off. He immediately placed both hands back on the wheel. "Is there anything you want to talk about, little sister? I might not have any answers, but I'm a pretty good listener."

"No."

As he continued driving, she began to wonder what he had in mind. He was obviously heading toward his parents' house, where he was staying while he was in town. Did he plan for him and her to play a rematch on the ping-pong table in the garage? Or would they climb over the mashed place in the fence onto the golf course for a midnight stroll? She couldn't really say what she wanted from him either, but it wasn't ping-pong. He had turned onto his street, and pulled over to the curb half a block shy of his parents' place.

"What are we doing?"

Robbie's fingers drummed the steering wheel. "I don't know. I wasn't even thinking about where I was going. Force of habit."

"I asked you to take me home. Did you have something else in mind?"

"Don't do this to me, little sister."

"I told you not to call me that."

"Okay. But I know how you get when one of these relentless moods hits you."

"You're avoiding the question. Did you have some agenda in cruising and then bringing me here?"

"Well, I thought you might want to walk around on the golf course."

"I don't."

He had the same old air of genial, easy confidence about him, a security about his humble place in the world that she'd always admired. He never seemed to agonize about anything, or set himself ambitions he couldn't attain with a few weeks of diligent concentration. His universe was a rational and friendly place. He went on the assumption that everyone else was, or could be, as straightforward and sunny as him. Often he used to say to her, I believe in the reasonable man theory. I believe if you're reasonable with people, they'll be reasonable with you. Apparently, his philosophy had worked for him up until now. No nasty, unpredictable accidents had fallen in his way so far. He took it for granted that he knew her, but he didn't. She gave him an accusing look. "If I hadn't happened to come back now, our paths might not have crossed for another five years. You didn't even tell me you'd gone off to be a river guide."

"Oh, so that's what this is all about. I didn't know I was supposed to. When people live in different places, sometimes they gradually get out of the habit of staying in touch, no matter how close they were before. It's not like you write me anymore either. Look, I don't want any hassles. If you want me to drive you home, I will. I think it's a big mistake to try to force ourselves to recover too much of a friendship in a few hours."

"Then why go traipsing through our old haunts? Am I supposed to get maudlin? Is this some sort of carpe diem thing?"

"No, of course not. That's not what I meant. Why are you so bitter about everything all of a sudden?"

"I might as easily ask you why you're so happy about everything. At least mine is a more natural state of being."

"Come onto the golf course with me and walk off a couple of those wicked white Russians. It's a pretty night. The stars are out. You need to start learning the names of the constellations. I've tried to teach you before, but you never pay any attention, because you figure you can always ask me to identify them. But I'm not always there, am I? Think of it this way—no matter where you go, the sky is always going to be there. And once you learn the constellations, you can enjoy them at your leisure. Even when you're by yourself."

"No thanks. I have too many solitary pleasures already."

He turned his head away for a moment, stung by her

bluntness. Then she felt his hand on her arm again. "Come on," he said, flashing her his most winning big brother grin. "I think my star chart is there in the glove compartment."

"I can't bear to walk around on the golf course. I want to stay in the car." She knew she was tormenting him unreasonably, even childishly, but she couldn't stop herself until the darkness that had settled over her, choking her, had spent itself. She could hardly even undertand the words she herself was speaking, as if uttering the nonsense language of a hex or a charm.

"Right. Well, whatever. It was only a suggestion." They sat in silence for several more moments. He tuned a few stations, then clicked the radio off again. "Country music is taking over the universe. It's even on Double Q. I can't believe Matt has gotten caught up in that junk too. Whenever I hear a pedal steel, all I can think of is Don Ho." He reached underneath his seat, extracted a brush, and started brushing his hair.

"Drive around," she said.

"That's all I've been doing for the past hour or so. Where do you want to go?"

"Drive around your neighborhood." The urgency in her voice made him silently obey. He put the car in gear and eased away from the curb. When he had traversed a few blocks, she reached over, unsnapped the shorts Robbie was wearing, and turned her body so she could work the zipper more easily.

"Hey, what the hell are you doing, Serena?"

"I'm just going to suck your cock." She could see from the rise in his shorts that he had gotten an instantaneous erection. As she worked them down around his hips, he lifted his bottom almost imperceptibly from the seat, and the shorts and his bikini underpants fell to his ankles above the accelerator pedal. She had neglected to mousse her hair, and she pulled a barrette from her pocket to clip to her bangs so they wouldn't get in the way. She took her time fastening the barrette, all the time keeping her eyes on his engorged penis, which stuck straight out between his legs. When she'd gotten herself situated, Serena leaned over and took the head of it into her mouth. It was scalding and dry, with a single drop of liquid at the tip, and throbbed lightly against her lips. Removing his penis from her mouth, she asked him if he could please put the seat back a couple of notches, because it was hard to fit her head underneath the wheel. He did as she asked.

"Listen, I can't—at least let me pull over. People don't really do this."

"Keep driving," she said. "You concentrate on your task, and I'll concentrate on mine. Is that a tilt wheel?"

"I'm not sure. My mother just bought this, and I don't know where everything is yet."

"It's okay. I'll make do." She took more of him into her mouth, as much as she could accommodate, making no effort to be delicate. She wanted to give him a real blow job, with no room for misinterpretation. From the sound of the road beneath the floorboards, it was obvious that his foot wasn't even on the accelerator. He was idling, playing it safe, like someone who has just secured his learner's permit and is gripped by a deathly fear of smashing into every single parked car he passes. The road must look six inches wide to him right now. She was deliberate, and made a lot of noise with her lips and tongue. It didn't take long for him to come.

As soon as she lifted her head, he swerved into someone's driveway and set the emergency brake.

"I don't think the car is going anywhere, Robbie. This isn't San Francisco."

He was in a big hurry to pull his shorts back up and get them fastened. She settled back into her bucket seat and searched through her purse for a pack of cinammon gum.

Once he had everything in its place, Robbie said, in as soothing a voice as he could manage, "It's okay. Everything's okay."

She chuckled as she took the foil off a stick of gum and popped it in her mouth. "Of course it's okay." From the solicitous way he was leaning over her, she could tell he expected her to be instantly filled with shame and remorse. Or maybe he was convinced that she had suffered temporary insanity, and he wanted to reassure her that he still respected her mind. "Relax, Robbie. For the record, I don't do that with everybody, in case that's what you're thinking. It was a special treat just for you." That remark seemed to shatter him completely. He had a look of utter astonishment on his face.

"I love you, Serena."

"You don't have to say that. In fact, I prefer that you don't say it."

"Well, what do you expect me to say? I'm having a lot of strong feelings right now."

"Say thank you, Serena, for a lovely time, and for the boutonniere. Tell me it's an evening you won't soon forget."

"You can pretend to be cynical if you want to, but to me this means something. This doesn't happen every day of the week. Not between us. If I had picked up some chick at High on Rose, that would be a different story."

"I see. You mean in that case you would have expected it."

"You know what I mean. We have a lot of past history together, and in five minutes all that has changed."

"Oh, Robbie, please, please don't start analyzing the shit out of this. Don't make more of it than is actually there. If it makes you feel more comfortable, think of it as a prank, like in the old days. You dared me to suck your cock, and I, not wanting to be thought less of a man than you, took up your dare. If you'd ever worked up the nerve to ask me to do this when we were fifteen, I probably wouldn't have hesitated, and afterward we would have smoked our Swisher Sweets and gotten sick to our stomachs. Not from the sin, or from the semen, but from the cheap tobacco."

"Yeah, that's a better way to think about it, I suppose." Robbie, his voice still quavering, collapsed into his seat and closed his eyes.

"Where did you say that star chart was? Maybe we should go walk around." All at once, the interior of the car felt dry and suffocating to her. In his frantic search for the tilt lever, perhaps he had accidentally turned on the defroster.

"In there somewhere. There's a map wallet, it could be inside one of the flaps." He switched on the overhead light so she could see better, and she reached up at once to switch it back off. She sensed that her face was flushed as well, and she didn't want to be the recipient of his searching gaze. "Here, let me look," he said. He leaned across the emergency brake and started to fish around, then changed his mind and began kissing her on the mouth. His arms encircled her as he eased his long body almost snakelike across the enclosed space. He was even stronger and more dexterous than he looked. The gentle but insinuating way he held and kissed her made her realize that he probably had a fair amount of experience with women, more than she'd counted on. Now he was kissing her long and deep, and even though she was enjoying it she pulled her mouth away because she didn't want him to get the wrong idea.

"We've got to go somewhere," he said, panting. "I want to be able to lie down next to you and stroke your face. How about if we check into a motel?"

She squirmed. The heavy feeling inside her had grown worse instead of dissipating. All she could think about was how to get away from him.

"Maybe that's not such a good idea. I thought you were supposed to meet Matt at JDI. Don't forget he's waiting for you."

"That's true. Well, he'll leave eventually if I don't show up. We're old buds, so he'll cut me some slack. I'll make it up to him later. He owes me one, anyway. I fixed the carburetor on his Chevy yesterday. Did you notice how smooth it was running?"

"Yes, it sounded great. Listen, why don't you drop me off now and go catch the last set of the Saddle Bangers with Matt? I'm kind of tired."

"You're not going brush me off so easily, Serena. You started this business, so don't act like I'm coming on to you all of a sudden. You knew exactly what you were doing."

"No, I didn't. It was an idea that popped into my idle head. Please, Robbie, be reasonable. Drop me off at home, and don't insist on coming in. I'm not being a tease. It's just that, well, to be straight with you, my life is really screwed up right now, and I don't think it's a good idea for you to become a part of it."

"Too late, little sister. I'm already a part of it."

They removed their shoes before entering. The house was quiet, with only a wakeful cat in the front hall sniffing about a potted plant. The floor squeaked with every tiptoed step. Not knowing her way around the house very well, she opened the door to a closet. The kitchen light was on.

A girl who looked vaguely familiar sat alone at the kitchen table with the chair pushed back, holding a piece of cold fried chicken over a cardboard box as she gnawed it, and reading the funny papers. Her body was hulking, and her head shaved. It took Serena a moment to recognize her as Deeann's baby sister, Bett, the unexpected child who Deeann's mother had carried to term at age forty, and who Serena and Deeann used to babysit for together. Bett had tweezed her eyebrows and drawn them back in with an eyebrow pencil in tilted slashes on each side that made Serena think of the *accent circonflex* in her old French grammar book. She wore fatigue pants. Except for the eyebrows, she might have been mistaken for a soldier on furlough.

She glanced up, and went back to the funnies.

"Hi, Bett. You've really grown up. I don't know if your sister told you, but I'm rooming with her now."

"Nah, she didn't mention it. I'm just crashing on her couch for tonight. When I came in a little while ago, she shouted from her room that she'd worked a double shift and had a splitting headache, and not to bring any of my friends in, because this wasn't the neighborhood flophouse. She thinks I'm a lesbian, and for her, that's the most horrible curse that could befall a woman. Hey, didn't you used to be a cheerleader, Serena?"

"No," answered Serena, a little indignantly. "What put that idea in your head?"

"I don't know. I thought you were on Deeann's squad. That's right, most of you guys were flower children. God, that seems like ancient history now. Was either of you all at Altamont? I thought it was so cool, the way they said Hell's Angels kept lobbing full cans of beer down on the crowd, and giving people concussions, and those hippies were so stoned, they thought the sky was falling, like Chicken Little. How stupid can you get? The stage diving here at the Vortex is so bogus. Everybody pretends like it's dangerous, but you know somebody is always going to catch you, because the club owner doesn't want a lawsuit. I heard in L.A. it's more authentic, because they let people drop sometimes. They must have insurance. By the way, somebody named Matt kept calling and asking for you. He was in a bar, so I couldn't hear him very well. He was shouting that he'd gotten free passes to someplace or other, and it was a dollar a pitcher until closing. He said he'd wait. That's not him there with you, is it?"

"I'd better go," said Robbie.

"No, I need you here," Serena whispered, and tightened her grip on his hand. "Bett, I'd like you to meet Robbie, a very old and cherished friend of mine. We go back quite a ways together."

"Is he your dude, or just a one-nighter?"

"And Robbie, this is Bett. I was her first babysitter. She had the hardest time going to sleep, so I used to rub her back and sing her Burl Ives songs."

"Oh yeah, I remember that. It was really soothing. Big rock candy mountain." Bett's sullen face brightened momentarily. "Wasn't Burl Ives one of the folk singers at Woodstock? Can you believe all those people just showed up for a three-day concert without bringing enough food for themselves? What were they thinking? I guess they believed manna was going to fall from heaven, or that there would be some kind of loaves and fishes thing. You all sure were trusting souls."

"Robbie and I are going to my room. We haven't seen each other for a long while, so we have a lot to talk about."

"I wish I had your luck," said Bett. "I don't score that often. Everybody thinks I'm a dyke, so the only ones who hit on me are women. The problem is, I don't really like women."

In bed, he was attentive. She had a suspicion that many of his sexual adventures had been silent couplings in tents with tawny sixteen-year-olds whose parents slept only yards away, then the very next day a tryst with the same girl's mother, after he had escorted her to the closest waterfall. He was the full-service guide, a low-key gigolo of the outdoors with a ready smile, healthy, robust, disease-free, so there could be no sense of sin or betrayal associated with any act involving him. Afterward, when their magical week on the Colorado had come to an end, the women would comment to their friends how a certain river guide had brought them out of themselves, or, in the case of the sixteen-year-olds, had made them a woman.

Not for him would be the neurotic types, the overanalyzing, self-lacerating, self-defeating nail-biters, but rather only women with strong calf muscles, capable of hefting a forty-pound backpack or humping on a narrow shelf of rock in the midst of a technical ascent, surrounded by chocks and carabiners and an ocean of air a thousand feet deep, women who believed in the immortality of their own bodies, or, in the case of the middle-aged, who lost their heads at a lower altitude, women who could be made to believe again for a moment in that immortality.

But with her, there was a sense of his wanting to go easy, missionary, slow. As he labored earnestly, looking at her with eyes full of honesty and feeling, reassuring her with his steadfast gaze that he had no salacious or disrespectful thoughts in his mind, she found herself unable to climax, or even to get very aroused. She wanted to be classified among the tawny immortals, while he wanted to erase the recent stain on their relationship.

When she realized there was going to be no orgasm for her this time, and that he was going to hold back on the off chance she might find her erotic center in the next five minutes, while he continued to scrutinize the minute shades of her response like a concerned camp counselor, she found herself wishing he would simply take his selfish pleasure, the way he damned well ought to under the circumstances. But in spite of herself, her arms and legs started to cling to him with a different sort of expectation. She wanted to shout for him to get off her, to stop condescending to her, but she found herself beginning to need him in precisely the way she assumed he wanted her to need him, and she half expected him to whisper in her ear the words "little sister," except that they would have been too incestuous, too unchaste.

After a time, he withdrew, without ejaculating, and pulled her across him. "It's okay," he said, again looking into her eyes with infinite comprehension. "I'm not expecting anything. It just feels good to be close."

Those were the very words she'd spoken any number of times over the years, to she didn't know how many men, including Skip, the men who for some reason or other couldn't always get it up with her. All of them had been attracted to her exotic good looks in the beginning, green eyes and blond hair, often assuming that she was of Scandinavian extraction, maybe Swedish if they were lucky, but when it came to the crunch, many of them had trouble performing. None of the men ever said so, but at bottom even the most liberated of them wanted a woman without too many complications, less verbal, less introspective, and what was worse was that she found herself wanting to be that woman. Still, she couldn't quite bring it off. She'd always had a strong libido, one that for the most part remained unsatisfied, while time and again she heard herself uttering that oldest of lies, It's okay, it just feels good to be close, to protect their egos so they could live to fuck another day, if not with her then with someone sunnier and perkier.

Now Robbie was saying those words to her, caressing her face, It's okay, taking care not to touch her erogenous zones for fear of bringing on performance anxiety, and the worst thing about it all was that he really meant what he was saying. It was okay with him. He didn't need the sex. He'd had his way with enough comely women that there doubtless was no sport left in the mere act. Now he was ready if necessary to make the ultimate sacrifice in order to achieve a more mature relationship.

Her mother had sometimes said to her, with the wicked

matronly killjoy knowingness of the middle-aged, who have already been where the next generation in line is doomed to go, that one day Serena would reach a point where stretching out in bed would feel just as good as doing it. Serena had vehemently denied that she would ever reach that point, because boredom came from simple lack of variety, not age per se. Now, however, she was beginning to wonder.

Serena's health had remained excellent so far, except for the swimmer's shoulder from too much diving in her teens and twenties, which meant that every morning for as long as she lived, she would have to stretch out the muscles around the popping, calcified socket. The pain, though constant, was so mild that most of the time she could ignore it. But even that single anatomical imperfection set her to imagining the gradual process of disintegration that had already begun within her body. The MRI report on her shoulder had come back using words like degeneration, arthritic, and even though the doctor, with his bookie's fondness for quoting odds, assured her that seven out of ten people were walking around with various states of degeneration and arthritis in their bodies without their even knowing it because they remained asymptomatic, she wondered why she couldn't be one of the other three, and she fretted over the fact that the damage, however slight, was irreversible. It wasn't like injured tissue that could repair itself. She carried around a mental image of her body as a skeletal X-ray filled with spots and discolorations in varying shades.

The odor left over from her and Robbie's lovemaking smelled to her all at once like the stench that came from between two molars if she neglected to floss for too many days. Robbie didn't seem to notice the smell, but perhaps that was because he had the aroma of sandalwood soap emanating from his own body. Maybe she had an overdeveloped bundle of olfactory nerves. In the past few weeks, on occasion, she sensed a pungency coming from her flesh much like that of her grandmother's when she had been bedridden at her parents' house near the end, and her mother kept having to turn her grandmother Lila in bed to keep bedsores from forming. When Serena had visited with Lila, she kept clutching Serena's hand, saying that there must be some mistake, because inside herself, she still felt twenty. As proof, she pointed to a picture on the wall of herself kissing her newlywed husband in a field of wheat. That's me, she said, trying to keep her voice from quavering. That's me. Serena had given her a sponge bath, an enema, fed her spoonfuls of vegetable soup, brought in a bunch of poppies, her favorite flower, which had always covered the hillside when she lived in the old house down in Middlesboro. When it was time for Serena to go, her grandmother held on as though the act of her granddaughter's leaving would siphon off the remaining youth in the room forever, leaving only the infirm and wizened body that she had been saddled with by accident.

"Everything okay? You seem distracted."

"It's fine. I'm a little tense, that's all."

"You want me to order a pizza or something? I can sit out on the front porch and wait for the delivery man so the doorbell won't wake up your roommate."

"I'm not hungry, but if you want one, I'm game."

"I just want you to be happy."

"Oh, I don't have any right to be unhappy. I'm really sorry for being in such a malicious mood when we were in the car. When I think of what Shar has been through, what do I really have to complain about? I'm getting adjusted to being here again, that's all."

"You made the right decision coming back. Sometimes you have to do something drastic to change your perspective. When all the campers were asleep, sometimes I'd slide out of my sleeping bag. I'm good at slipping in and out of places without making any noise. You know where I would go?"

"I don't think I'll guess."

"Come on, just take a stab."

"Visiting."

"Visiting?" He laughed. "Who would I visit, with everybody asleep in their tents? No, I'd take a night swim in the river by myself, when I felt myself getting too complacent, too routine.

We weren't supposed to, because of insurance, but I couldn't resist. Did you ever do that, swim at night alone?"

"Yes. A couple of days ago, in fact."

"See, I knew you would say yes. That's something else we have in common. What was it that drew you there?"

"An irresistible urge."

"How would you describe it?"

"No, you say. It's your story."

"I want to feel the rush of the current against me, while I hold onto a tough tree root. It makes me feel more alive. Everybody says I take too many chances, and it's true I push the edge. But I know my limits. I'm not like those three guys who drowned that I told you about. I'm so familiar with that river, I'm not going to do myself any harm. See, I want to live for a long time, so I take calculated risks, just enough to keep my juices flowing. I never get into a situation I can't handle. I don't know whether those guys had a death wish, or whether they were stupid."

"It sounds to me like they had bad luck."

"Maybe. Sometimes, though, I think there are no accidents. When people are down on themselves, they find a way to make bad things happen to them."

"Why do you want to be with me, Robbie?"

"Isn't it enough to tell you I'm in love with you? Do I have to have a reason?"

"Yes."

"Okay, because you're smart and tough."

"No, I'm not. I promise you that I'm neither."

"You are. We've known each other for a long time. You're being modest, that's all. I had to hook up with all kinds of women to realize that all along, you were the person. I'll never forget those conversations we had on the way up to Michigan, when we went with Matt. I haven't had that kind of conversation with any other female since."

"I don't remember anything we said to each other on that trip." He flinched, but kept his eyes on her. "I'm not saying that to be mean. I've tried to remember the exact words, many times, but I can't."

"It doesn't make any difference. I remember it. Only one of us has to be the oral historian. I'm frustrated with women who have to live their lives through me. They don't mean to, but they get so dependent."

"I'm dependent. I'm just like all those other women, only worse, because I do mean to be that way. I have to, in order to survive. That means I'll end up sucking you dry."

"I don't know whether you're trying to insult me, or if it's this funny mood of yours, but I wish you'd stop talking that way. I'm trying to woo you, and you're not making it very easy. I don't know exactly what I'm supposed to say. I'll be honest—usually, me and women don't speak this much. "

"You know why I'm saying all this? First, because it's true. Second, because I'm falling for you too. I don't know when it happened, maybe in the last ten minutes. That's why I want to get all this out up front, so you won't have any regrets later."

"You're not scaring me off."

"What I wouldn't give to be a creampuff. If we decide to do this, I want it to be for keeps. I don't mean getting married, but staying together. There's too little of me left to waste on things that don't lead anywhere. Once it starts, I'm not going to leave you, and I'm not going to let you leave me."

"Hey, that's exactly what I want. Women assume I'm a one-night type of dude, but they're mistaken. In my soul, I'm monogamous. I'm the opposite of Jimmy Carter. I've been thinking I would look around for some engineering work in town and try to give Matt a hand with his farm idea. If that will help Shar and Matt get through, I'm willing. It's not like I have a master plan. I can as well work here as somewhere else. To tell you the truth, I won't mind getting away from that guide stuff. The river running isn't as much fun as it used to be. With so many outfits competing for the tourists, the river has gotten crowded. What do you think?" He was smiling at her, relaxed, already making himself at home, relieved they didn't have to talk serious for too long at a stretch, just enough to keep the juices flowing. Part of him still felt that they were sitting back in the old concrete pipe, drinking cream ale. "I've always thought of you as a potential earth mother. I'll bring back to the farmhouse strings of quail for you to dress. Maybe we'll turn into survivalists. Teach our kids at home, stop paying taxes, tell the government to go to hell, outwit the revenooers by growing our marijuana in clever places, turn the root cellar into a bomb shelter."

"I can't answer right now. Everything has happened too fast."

"Sure, let's take our time. There's no big hurry, as long as Shar stays in remission. I don't know all the details, but Matt seems to think they fixed the problem, so I'm optimistic. The important thing for now is that you and I bared our souls to each other. As long as people keep secrets from each other, they can't really be soulmates. Maybe I will order that pizza."

She was awakened by the metallic sound of banging. Then a voice hollered "Cut that hubbub out! I've got a hangover. " It wasn't clear to her where she was. The side of her body closest to the wall was clammy with sweat. Her throat constricted, but she kept her eyes open, attempted to breathe, and took in the details of the room. She tried to sit up, but couldn't. The fan in the doorway helped her locate herself. That voice was Bett complaining about her hangover. She felt blindly for Robbie behind her, but he wasn't in bed anymore.

The dream started to come back to her. She had been sitting in the grass next to the wooden back porch of a farmhouse, overlooking a field of poppies, wearing a granny skirt, with a baby cradled in the patch of skirt between her knees. She was waiting for the baby's father, the man she'd worked for as a nanny. It wasn't clear whether the baby was hers, or whether she had been brought there as a wet nurse. A sow slid out from beneath the porch, teats dragging in the dirt, and began to eat the soapsuds that had spilled over the side of the tub. As its snout sniffled along the trail of suds, the sow's hefty side kept banging against the metal tub. She wished the noise would stop. The baby had started to fuss because it was hungry, and she felt the letdown in her breasts. She let go of the baby to unbutton her blouse. When the sow got close, it snatched up the infant between its jaws and ran off on its short little legs with surprising speed.

Throwing on her terry robe and lurching to the doorway, she knocked the fan on its side. Its grate vibrated urgently against the wood floor until she wrestled it back upright. In the kitchen, Deeann, silk robe cinched about her, stirred a pot of oatmeal. Her hair was brushed, and she had applied her make-up. She was strict as an Egyptian woman under the purdah in never allowing herself to be seen without makeup. Deeann always began her day with what she referred to as her bowl of gruel, because it was supposed to clarify the skin. "Oh, Deeann, it's you. I thought somebody was breaking into the house."

Deeann calmly surveyed her roommate. "You look like hell, Serena."

"I thought you said I looked fabulous."

"That was yesterday. I'm going to have to teach you something about makeup. You're a winter person."

"A winter person?"

"Remember, even corpses don't have to look like corpses if they have the right makeup job. Did I tell you I have a cosmetician friend who works part time over at the mortuary giving makeovers for three hundred bucks a pop? Apparently they can't find many cosmeticians willing to do it. She says it's great, because unlike most of her clients, they lie perfectly still and don't complain. Can you tell me why there's a catbox in the bathroom? I nearly passed out when I went in there to put on my face. Bett swears she didn't have anything to do with it."

"Isn't that your cat?"

"You must be joking. I'm allergic to cats. They're murder on my contacts."

"Oh, yeah. I remember now. I found a stray yesterday in the alley. It didn't have any tags and half its tail had been cut off, so

I figured it was a stray. It looked like it needed a home. I can't stand to see animals mistreated. I must have gone out and bought some kitty litter."

"You're going to have to get rid of it. This isn't the SPCA. You should have asked me. If there's one thing I can't stand, it's the stench of a catbox. I like all the rooms in my house to smell feminine and nice."

"It's a female cat."

"They're the worst. We can talk about maybe keeping her as an outdoor pet, but she'll have to be neutered right away. Otherwise, once she's in heat, we're going to have every male cat in the neighborhood prowling around our front door, drawn by the scent." She whacked the metal spoon against the side of the pan to dislodge a glob of oatmeal. "Speaking of which, Bett tells me you had a friend over last night."

Serena had her shaking under control. She looked over to the coffeepot, but like her mouth, it was dry. "True. Don't you have residents sleep over?"

"No, I don't. First of all, I don't put out much," she said, giving Serena a significant look. "Usually it isn't worth it. If word gets around the hospital that I'm easy, I'm not going to be able to do my job as clinical supervisor. And besides, on the rare occasions when I do, I make the man take me over to his place. That seems better etiquette to me. Their apartments are usually a disaster, but I'm not going to have the neighbors making comments about my personal life. "

"But you go out to see male strippers with your girlfriends."

"That's different. The man has his clothes off, but all of us are dressed. That's the ideal situation, as far as I'm concerned. Did you go down on him?"

"What?"

"Did you give him head?"

"I'm not going to answer that question."

"Why not? You always told me in the old days. Anyway, you don't have to. I can guess the answer. And I'll bet he took off in the middle of the night, after you fell asleep. He probably told you he was going out onto the porch to smoke or something, and then he disappeared. He knows he'll get what he wants when he wants, so you don't have any leverage over him."

"I don't want to discuss this anymore. That's not how I conduct my romances. I go by feeling."

"The worst possible strategy. Oh, I know you think I'm a mercenary, but Serena, all relationships are contracts. That's no news to anybody. You're only cheating yourself if you don't make the terms explicit. Take off your robe and let me give you a massage. You look like you're working on a heart attack."

"You want to give me a massage?"

"Sure, like we always did in high school. I think the baby oil is in that lower cabinet. I try to do this for my patients who can't sleep when I can find the time, which isn't often. It works so much better than giving them sleeping pills. Let's go in the living room." On the couch was a rumpled blanket, but no Bett, who appeared to have left the house in protest. "Here, let me help you off with that. Your breasts have stayed nice. Not big, but firm. Your butt and stomach are tight, and no cellulite. You can't believe how many women our age have let themselves go. You've got the body of a nineteen-year-old. I'm jealous. Lie down on the carpet." A warm thread of oil poured onto Serena's back and snaked down the crevice in the middle. Deeann's fingers stopped the stream, and spread it in an even coat over her skin.

"You're a lot better looking than I am, there's no question about it, and you could have anybody you want, but the difference is, I know how to handle myself. Last year, a millionaire named J. B. Madden proposed to me. He has a big horse farm over in Frankfort. He was on the unit as my primary with a mild infarction, nothing serious, but it shook him up. He realized there wasn't much he could do with all his millions if he had a massive one." Her fingers gently prodded, finding trigger points, and little by little worked deeper into the muscles. Taking a deep breath, Serena let air flow down into her body, into her extremities, the oxygen an ice blue color, then out again, the carbon dioxide darkening into black as it brought out the impurities. "He invited me down to the Virgin Islands, to play at the casinos, snorkel, sunbathe. I told him I'd go, but only under the condition that we have separate rooms. He balked at that. He said if I really loved him, I wouldn't set preconditions. He said I was trying to take advantage of him, but I told him it was the other way around."

The tightness in her abdomen was slowly being replaced by a tingle as Deeann's fingers explored the subtle muscles between her ribs, moving down one by one on either side, as if she were looking for a particular rib, the missing rib. The diffuse arousal left over from last night started gathering itself again. She visualized Robbie's hands stroking her, only this time she wasn't freezing up. "So, what happened when you told him that?"

"We went and took separate rooms. Both of us had a blast. Windsurfing, snorkeling, parasailing. He couldn't do the real strenuous stuff, of course, but he had fun watching me do it. It made him feel back in the world. He told me afterward that it was the best money he'd ever spent."

"But you didn't sleep with him?" Serena lay absolutely still, as still as one of those corpses being made over at the mortuary, as the tension bottled up inside her gathered itself for release.

"What do you take me for? I'm not a golddigger. Of course I slept with him, two nights, in his room. He was very sweet, attentive. Some of the best sex I've had, in fact. When they get that age, they know they can't wow you with their bodies or their gymnastics, so they really try hard. But frankly, I don't think he could have stood more than two nights with me. I took his pulse before and afterward. I was his nurse, after all, and I felt an ethical responsibility not to land him back in the hospital. I do a lot of teaching with my coronary patients so they'll realize that a heart attack doesn't have to mean the end of their sex life, as long as they know how to be moderate."

The feeling of pleasure was beginning to quicken, but she had become self-conscious again, and was afraid she would lose it by panicking. She lingered at the threshold, then squeezed her eyelids shut to push herself over with a deep sigh. Deeann handed Serena her robe. "There, that ought to refresh you. Can I serve you some oatmeal? God, isn't this great to be in our own little kitchen? I feel like we're two sorority girls without a housemother."

"Sure," said Serena, picking at a hangnail she hadn't quite chewed off. "Oatmeal sounds nice." She was trying her best to sound matter of fact instead of breathy. "So, you didn't give him an infarction."

"No," said Deeann, climbing onto a stepstool and taking two matching bowls down from the cabinet. She smiled a brilliant, girlish smile. "I got his heart rate going pretty good, but like I said, I know when to stop."

When they were situated at the breakfast table, Deeann unfolded the morning paper, and handed one of the back sections to Serena. They ate in silence as they read. There had been another explosion in one of the mines down near Hazard. Serena's grandfather Byrd had worked for many years as a coal miner before she was born, until he got black lung. He spent twelve or fourteen hours a day sleeping, and the rest of the time he whiled away on the screened-in porch, drawing long, mournful breaths and reading books by Louis L'Amour, wearing a pair of eyeglasses he'd bought off a rack at a drugstore. Nobody could make him go to the eye doctor. When Serena went down to stay with them in the summer, Lila's sister would come over for supper twice a week, and after the two women had done the dishes and let her help dry, they would all retire to the porch to eat fresh blackberry cobbler, Byrd's favorite, even though the seeds gave him irritable bowel. They'd sit feeling the air stir from time to time, until nothing was visible down the hillside except the intermittent lights of the fireflies and the unbroken black silhouettes of conifers. Serena would position herself next to Byrd's chair on a cane-bottom footstool, one he'd made himself, with knife scratches in the legs. He would take out his false teeth to entertain her, or make asides about the two sisters' conversation, as if he and she were in an opera box watching a performance.

"Women are catty," he'd say to her under his breath. "Catty to the bone. You see, the men don't have to keep them in check, because they do a pretty good job by theirselves. But don't tell your grandmother that, or she might mend her ways, and then where would I be?"

Lila and Serena's great-aunt Betsy would inevitably be discussing the travails of such and such a woman they knew, whose husband had left her and the children, or who was rumored to be loose, or who had contracted one disease or another. Inevitably, at the end of their joint recitation of the facts of the case, one of them would shake her head, cluck her tongue, and say, "Well, she brought it on herself. She brought it on herself." Lila and Betsy were as pious, categorical, and unforgiving in their judgments as Old Testament prophets.

During one of those sessions, Byrd bent down to Serena with a glint in his eye and said, "Did I ever tell you about the two cats who clawed their way to heaven? Once two boys was a-hunting and when they come out of the woods down by the river bank, a wildcat was waiting. Both cocked their guns and fired right at the same time and kilt her, and she rolled into the river. Two little girlie cats come out of the woods, and those boys grabbed aholt of them, put them in a sack. Got that mama cat out of the water and skinned her. Eachun got hisself a cat, but they couldn't settle on who would get the mother wildcat's hide. So they agreed that each would keep his cat for six months, and they'd fix a meeting place for the cats to fight it out, and find out which could whip the other one. Whoever's cat won would take that hide for theirself, you see. When the time come, each feller put his cat on top of the smokehouse to fight. They fit and they fit, but neither could outfight the other one. The cats wouldn't give in nor back down the roof none, so the only way to go was up. They clawed to the top of the roof, and clawed right on until they went up into the air and soon out of sight. Fur was falling all over creation. Finally, those boys went away and when they come back six months later, in the dead of winter, the fur was still falling like snow. They could see it was no use waiting for those two female cats to finish, so they finally just give up, went on home and give the old mother hide away to the first person they saw."

"I hear that," said Lila. "I hear what you're saying. Don't listen to him, sugar. He's telling you another whopper. Trying to turn you agin your own kind, and our side needs all the recruits we can get."

"Well," said Byrd, laughing his wheezy laugh, "if she don't want to hear stories, she ought not of sot down here next to me. She brought it on herself."

"Deeann, have you ever thought about living on a farm?"

"Don't you remember, I lived on one until I was ten, up in a horrible little mountain place called Mousie. Those were the worst years of my life. Watching my father butcher puny little pigs that didn't have any more meat on them than our dog, and me having to pull out the innards." When Deeann said "innards," Serena could hear the backcountry twang creep into her voice. "We ate chitterlings until I thought I'd bust. The best thing that ever happened to me was when my parents moved to Lexington so Daddy could work in a tool and die factory. Otherwise I would have ended up a hillbilly. We used to belong to a Primitive Baptist church, where the women can only talk to God through the men. That part wasn't a total waste, though. At least it gave me training for working with surgeons."

She hadn't been in the alternative school for more than five minutes before a child sat in her lap, and another one had hold of her pants. On reaching adulthood, she hadn't at first paid any particular mind to children, but they had a natural attraction to her. The lesson she learned right off was that you didn't befriend children; rather, they chose you for their own inscrutable reasons, ones you had little say over. At that age, both the boys and the girls had an intuition about which people they could bring safely into their world. Sometimes their guilelessness would allow them to get tricked, but not nearly as often as adults imagined.

The younger children crowded around a glass-enclosed terrarium from which a guinea pig was being lifted. Many little hands reached for it in unison, but the guinea pig, rather than growing alarmed, had gone immediately limp, only its nostrils quivering. The guinea pig seemed to have grown used to this genial hazing, and to have decided that the best way to survive the daily ritual was to give itself over completely without trying to escape. The children tried their best to be delicate as each passed a finger over the animal's back, but every so often an over-enthusiastic finger would apply enough pressure to squeeze the body down so it looked like it was being rolfed.

The little girl in her lap was telling a story about a woman who had caught a fish with her hands in the creek, made it into a pet, and taught it to walk on dry land on its fins. The fish got so attached to the woman that it would follow her around everywhere she went, like a puppy, and it even slept at the foot of her bed at night. Nobody could have loved or obeyed its master more than the fish, who never let the woman go out of her sight. If the woman was making supper, the fish would sit on top of the table and keep her company. When she planted corn in her field, the fish walked right along beside her in the furrow. Even when she walked down to the outhouse, the fish would wait patiently outside for the woman to finish her business. Everything went along very well between the two of them, until one day the woman had to reach the other side of the creek to see a granny midwife to give her a cure for a bad rash. To get to the other bank, the woman and the fish had to cross over a bridge made of planks. The bridge had gaps between the rough planks, and when the fish tried to hop from one plank to the next, it slipped between the cracks, fell into the creek, and drowned.

"That's not true," said one of the older boys, ceasing work on his tinkertoy space station long enough to roll his eyes. "Fish can't really walk."

"It could so if it was a magic fish," one of the girls responded.

"What's an outhouse?"

"It's where you go *poo poo*," another girl answered with

enthusiasm. "Your poo poo falls all the way down through the world and devils use it for coal to make their fire hotter."

"It does not. It goes to China. Everybody knows that."

"Well, is it a magic fish?"

"Yeah, is it?"

"I don't know. My dad told me that story."

"Poor fish," said one boy who had about him the precociously melancholy look of a poet. "He wouldn't have drowned if somebody had sanded down the planks on the bridge so they fit together better. We have an electric sander, and it planes off doors right good."

"I wish I had a fish like that," said another boy. "I had a Siamese fighting fish in my fishbowl, but my Mom only allowed me to have one, so it died. When Siamese fighting fish don't have somebody to fight with, they get lonesome and die. I dumped food in there all the time, but it didn't have any appetite."

"Did you flush it down the toilet? I wonder if toilets go all the way down to the devil too."

"To China," said the tinkertoy engineer with quiet authority.

"We had a memorial service but she made me flush it. She said the cat would go crazy smelling it and trying to dig it up. When I flushed, the fish swirled around and around faster and faster, and all of a sudden it disappeared. It was pretty cool. I do kind of miss it, though. I forgot to give it a name."

"Oh no," one of the little girls cried out. She seemed genuinely distressed. "That means it will go to hell."

"No, it won't. Are you Catholic or something?"

"Yes, I am. My mom said not everybody has to be Baptists in this lousy godforsaken town."

"Hey," said the young poet, brightening up. "Wouldn't flushing it down the commode be sort of like baptising it?"

"In our congregation," the girl said huffily, "we sprinkle water over everybody's head. I saw them do it to a baby a couple of weeks ago."

"Well, in our church, the pastor puts on really long rubber boots and there's kind of like this big aquarium behind the place where he talks, except you can't really see it. Then he walks down into it with whoever the person is, holds their nose, and ducks their head back in the water, and you can see them stand up trying to get their breath back. They don't let us take Jesus Christ as our personal Lord and Savior until we're like nine or something, so I haven't done it. I guess they think we might drown."

"What happens if you die before you get baptized?" asked the Catholic girl.

"I don't know." Everyone looked uneasy. "I wonder what really did happen to the Siamese fighting fish, and that other fish that drowned? Teacher, where did they go?"

"I'm sure they're probably in heaven," said Serena. "Fish heaven, that is. It's a different place from where we go, because animals like to be with other animals." She was appalled to hear herself saying these things. But she honestly couldn't come up with any better explanation than the one she'd always promised she wouldn't give when this moment came. Maybe there really was an animal heaven, for all she knew. Besides, she didn't want to lose her job on the first day by creating religious controversy. Her father had no end of trouble with the literalists in the Southern Baptist Convention, the ones who wanted to shrink human history into three thousand years, so she knew where that path led. She was back in serious Bible country.

A man in Mount Sterling who'd developed five cancerous tumors had prayed for the Lord to remove them, and within a few weeks, they dissolved. He had gone out and started his own church in order to repay God for the miracle that had been granted. When the lay preacher had run into Carson in the grocery recently, he'd told him that he needed to have more faith and pray harder if he really wanted his affliction removed. He'd said I'm going to put you in my prayers, Brother Carson, but you've got to jump on the prayer train if you want it to work for you. Brother Carson, not even Pastor Carson. In spite of her agnosticism, it irked Serena that the man hadn't had the decency to refer to him as Pastor.

She wished she'd been there when it happened so she could have given the man a good belt in the mouth. Her father, of course, had remained perfectly polite and good-natured, and thanked the man for remembering him in his prayers. She could see him leaning on his cane, smiling, nodding, as the talk turned to comparing the prices and quality of pork ribs. You can't buy this cheap marked down stuff. Get you a good cut now, and you pay a little more but it ain't got so much fat so it don't all burn up on the grill. Here, here's five dollars, and I want you to put that right back on the shelf and you take you this one here. No, no, this one's on me, the Lord's been good to me this year, and I want to do it. And Carson would end up taking the five dollars and letting the man exercise his hard-won magnanimity. Carson never stopped performing his ministry for a single moment, and he would be quick to spot the glimmer of fear and uncertainty, the haggardness that never quite went away, even from the eyes of someone who had been the recipient of a miracle. Once they'd had a glimpse of death, however brief, they never forgot. He knew that perhaps the man had fallen behind in his tithing over the years, in the days before he'd become a lay preacher, and Carson wasn't going to be an impediment to the man's attempt to make up for lost time by buying a package of pork ribs for a fellow sufferer in this vale of sorrow.

Carson would give the man a hearty slap on the shoulder, say Me and Josie are sure going to enjoy these ribs tonight, she's home right now making a blackberry cobbler. You come on out to Chalk Lake, and let me give you some of the zucchini the ladies in my congregation keep pawning off on me. You have to be careful in town this time of year. If you're running errands and forget to lock your car, when you return the back seat will be all filled up with zucchini. Mount Sterling used to be a safe place, but it's sure going to the dogs.

"My fish really did go to heaven?" asked the boy, turning teary with gratitude. For this hour at least, Serena was the final word, the arbiter, their alpha and their omega.

"I'm sure he's safe. Maybe he won't feel so lonesome now. Maybe he found somebody to fight with."

" A friend of yours is on the phone. I told him it's late, but he said he has to talk with you now."

"Okay. Tell him I'll be right there." When Deeann had gone, Serena slid the cat out from beneath the covers, where it had been nestling against her leg. Unhooking the screen, she dropped it to the ground, where it yowled in protest several times before giving up and scampering off into the darkness, toward whatever nighttime haunts it had discovered during its times of exile. She envied its ability to climb a tree, find a comfortable branch and settle itself anew. In a few moments, it would have forgotten that it had been sleeping next to her, and wouldn't come around again until sometime in the morning, when it started to get hungry. She, on the other hand, would feel all night long the lack of its fur against her outer thigh.

Whenever she didn't have a human next to her, she had an animal, and when she didn't have an animal, she had a stuffed animal. All her life she had kept a stuffed animal around to sleep with. It was a mystery to her why other people voluntarily gave up that particular comfort of childhood. The only thing that had changed was that as a child, she had been attached to a particular alligator, whereas now, it didn't matter which of her stuffed animals she took off her shelf, as long as there was one in bed with her when the need arose.

"Serena, it's me, Matt. I know it's late, but I've got some news that I knew you'd want to hear. I sold one of my songs."

"Fantastic. Who to?"

"A new independent outfit. Aggressive and growth oriented. They actually called me on the phone. The president and CEO of the company said the tune was very catchy."

"I'm really proud of you. Who's going to record it?"

"They didn't quite say. It's still in the development stage. But I'm getting an advance, so I'll have some money to put on the down payment for the farm. I think we should all go out and look at it. I talked to Robbie a little while ago, and he's psyched."

"How much money did you make?"

"Well, they wanted to give me five thousand dollars to buy the song outright, but I told them no. So we agreed on two thousand, and a percentage of the net profits. They'll be sending me a contract in a couple of weeks. See, I know a little bit about the business. If one of your songs hits big, you can make a million dollars. It's happened many a time. And you know, Willie Nelson and Carole King both got their start as songwriters, and look where they are."

"Where *is* Carole King?"

"I don't even care if I become a big star. I'll be happy just to become one of those Nashville tunesmiths. And I've got plenty of songs ready, so I won't be short on my supply. Maybe I can work on the side as a studio musician, kind of a Chet or Vassar type thing."

"But you don't actually know whether or not it's going to be recorded?"

"You told me yourself when I played it for you that you thought it would be a big hit."

"Well, yes, I'm sure it will be. But we can't base a thirty-year mortgage on that expectation."

"Ten-year mortgage. I did some calculations, and we can save a hundred thousand bucks over the long haul. We bite the bullet, and by the time we all hit our midlife crisis, we'll own the farm outright, and we can spend our money on trips to the Keys. Do the Jimmy Buffet thing once a year. Robbie says he can rustle up a couple of thou, and I've persuaded Shar to part with the same amount, as long as everybody else does. I know you don't have a lot of cash, but when my money starts rolling in, I'll give you back your share. Don't you want to live with Robbie? You've got to pin that boy down, Serena, get his money tied up in a long-term deal where he can't pull it out whenever he wants to, or next thing you know he'll be back out on the Colorado River."

"You think he'd do that to me?"

"It doesn't have anything to do with you. But I know him too well. If the situation is undefined, he'll start to get restless. Right now the boy is so lovesick I'm thinking of writing a song about it. There's so many of those gamblin' ramblin' songs, they need to have one about a fellow who stays put, just to kind of balance things out."

"He doesn't act lovesick."

"Maybe not the same way you would. But when Robbie cuts his hair, dresses up, and takes a regular job, he's damn sure not doing it for me. That engineering shit is going to wear him down quick, unless he feels he's got a reason for doing it."

"You really think he took the job for me? He said he wanted to help you and Shar out."

"Think it? I stone cold know it. He won't go it unless we're a foursome."

"Okay, I'll ride over with you all just to have a look. But I don't want to get in over my head."

"You're already in over your head. Only question now is how far down in the deep end you're willing to go."

The farm was set off a rural route, behind fieldstone fences built around the time of the Civil War. The farmer told them nobody built fences like that any more, partly because it would cost a fortune for the labor alone, even if you could find a quarry with stone slabs of that quality. You couldn't ask niggers to haul it around, them days was long over, and there wasn't much convict labor to be leased out any more. Only two or three fellows in the whole Southeast knew how to repair fences of that kind, real artisans, and they must make a pretty good living, but the secret was going to die with them. He didn't know why in the hell these young people didn't learn good trades like caning and furniture making and stonemasonry. He was glad to see a bunch of young folks like theirselves willing to take a gamble on farming, it was a hard life but a noble one, if the damn subsidies hadn't fluctuated so much he would have been able to make it. He was

CHALK LAKE 〜 72

giving it to them dirt cheap, a hundred and forty thousand dollars for nearly two hundred acres of land. The farmhouse, all the outbuildings, everything had been kept in good repair because he was meticulous, but part of the problem was you couldn't hire good help like you could twenty years ago. The few hired hands who would work for a wage came and went as they pleased, plumb in the middle of topping tobacco, when the weather got too hot to suit them, they'd take off down to Kentucky Lake and go trout fishing, and the rest of them nogoods ran up and down the road with their hotrods wasting gasoline when they could be earning a living wage. Nobody was reliable, so he'd leased out the tobacco rights the last few years, you could make a little income off that, but he was getting too old to work it all himself; even his wife, who'd been a real helpmeet to him, had passed on and it just didn't seem worth it no more. He never had been nervous in his life, not the fretful type, always slept good soon as his head hit the piller, never had truck with doctors until a couple of years ago, but now they had him on some kind of sleeping pill, he didn't even know what it was called and didn't want to know. It wasn't a natural sleep, though, because it gave him too many peculiar dreams. They were always trying to explain to him this condition and that condition he had, but he didn't want to know anything about it, they were the specialists, so just give him the pills and he'd try to remember to take them. He'd advise them to lease out the rights, or try to work out some kind of sharecrop arrangement, because if the truth be told the four of them didn't look too much like farmers to him. He was letting it go for a song, because if he didn't he'd have to file for bankruptcy, he was being straight out honest with them, and it would kill him to see it auctioned off by the bank, but he had his pride, so he wasn't going to dicker with them, one forty, a good fair price, on the low side, take it or leave it, and besides he had to buy himself a little place in one of these towns around here, he didn't have anybody to do for him anymore, and all he knew how to cook was breakfast, his cholesterol was too high but he just couldn't give up bacon, you didn't eat it for seventy plus years and all of a sudden stop because some doctor who didn't look in too good a health himself told you to, besides if he did take that advice, sure as shooting the next year they'd publish an article in the paper saying the doctors had decided after all that eating bacon fat helped keep you from getting heart disease. They was always changing their mind about them things. He didn't have that much time left, but what time he did have he was going to spend it eating bacon. The years had taken away not only his farm, but married life and whisky and tobacco and pert near everything else he enjoyed, they'd castrated him a couple of years ago, he'd done a lot of gelding and castrating in his day, but he never expected to be on the receiving end of it. Now bacon was all he had left in the way of pleasure, and he'd probably keel over chewing on a piece of it, which suited him just fine. The four of them were lucky they had somebody to care for them and about them. He missed his wife something awful, God bless her soul, she made the flakiest biscuits on this earth, not these ones that popped out of a can like a trick snake in a novelty shop, and he thought about her every day, and prayed for her at night when he lay in their bed under the blanket she'd quilted for their wedding. In spite of her arthritis she'd quilted and crocheted right up to the end. These two young couples should cleave unto each other the way him and his wife had, that was his advice if they'd permit an old man to speak a word of advice. Him and his wife had had a good life together and this generation could too, the four of them could do it on this farm, the land was a little on the rocky side, he wasn't going to lie to them, but he'd raised tobacco, corn, soybeans, and a bit of everything on it, it would yield good if you worked it right. He'd maintained everything in the house real good, the original plumbing had been replaced with copper pipe, they was no way they could expect a better bargain than he was offering them, but he would at least get some satisfaction out of knowing that his sorrow would be their luck, there was some comfort in that, rather than having the bank foreclose and give it away to some person who wouldn't take the kind of care of it that he had. They had to promise him that, that they would put their heart and soul into it.

"We're not going to change a thing," Serena found herself saying, speaking for the group. "We plan to leave it just the way it is."

"In that case," said the farmer, "I can have my lawyers draw up the papers for you right away. You all can move in at the beginning of the month if ye like."

"Lawyers?" said Matt. "You have more than one lawyer?"

"Aw, no. That's just a figure of speaking. Everybody says that around here. He does put John C. Miller and Associates on his letterhead, but he's the only one in the office, unless you count the janitor who cleans up at night."

After a supper of porkchops, Serena's father lay in the recliner to rest his eyes. She and her mother retreated to the screened-in porch. They hulled black walnuts for the cakes her mother was making for a church bake sale. Since Carson's diagnosis of cancer, Josie had, without making any mention of it, given in gradually to the role of pastor's wife, and had started doing little things like taking a turn at the Sunday school nursery or helping out with church bazaars. She wondered whether her mother had actually started to believe in God—one, that is, besides the stone goddess.

In the porchlight below them, Serena could make out the statue. The only deity Josie had ever worshipped was the earth goddess her friend Therese had sculpted for her many years ago, when the two women were still young. It sat beside the walk just beyond the patio. The pores of the earth goddess's stone skin had grown bigger over time as the rain continued to pour down on her head. She had hairline cracks from being dropped by movers and was covered with lime green moss, like the skin of scum that grew around the docks of Chalk Lake in the summertime.

"Remember that you and Dad were willing to buy this

cabin sight unseen? It was nothing except a good feeling you had. Aren't you happier here than anywhere you've ever been?"

"I do like it, that's a fact."

"The farmer says he's got an allotment of three acres that can be put into tobacco, or the rights can be leased."

"Well, at least that's something. You'd derive some income off it, then."

"I'm not sure whether or not we'll lease the acreage. Not everybody feels good about making money off tobacco."

"But you smoke."

"Actually, Matt is the one who's most against it."

Josie cocked an eyebrow. "Considering all the substances Matt has smoked over the years, he doesn't have much room to be critical of the tobacco industry."

"Yeah, I know. Shar's for it. And I have to come up with my portion of the down payment soon. Two thousand dollars."

"You know Carson doesn't condone people living together out of wedlock. He'd like to see you married. But your father said he would take a second mortgage on the cabin."

"I don't want to ask you for that."

"I know you don't. It's a decision we made. Just don't disappoint Carson. He loves Robbie. So make it last."

Everything felt all at once very easy between herself and her mother. Serena could hear the electric bug zapper eliminating insects in the darkness below, and its familiarity made the sound comforting. They extracted the meats and tossed the shells into the bucket in a quiet, conspiratorial way. Josie chuckled low in her throat.

"What?"

"Oh, it's nothing. Back when I was carrying you, I had an obstetrician of the old school. There were no birthing rooms like they have nowadays, or LaMaze classes. They pretty much hoisted me into the stirrups and I went along for the ride. My doctor told me what to eat, how much weight I was supposed to gain, and when the time came, he put me under heavy sedation. I fought him the whole way as best I could, but I was young and I'd never had a baby before, so I more or less had to go along with most of his bullying in the end. He used to get a squint-eyed look on his face when he was about to dispense weighty medical advice. 'Josie,' he said to me one morning, and the razor burns on his neck were as red as gills, 'I advise against you trying to breast feed this baby. I know you're dead set on it, and hard-headed as a ball peen hammer, and nothing I say is going to make the slightest bit of difference to you. But you don't have the patience for it, and there's no use putting yourself through the aggravation.' Breast feeding wasn't too much in favor at that time. I don't know, I guess they looked on it as a backwoods practice, and all the young mothers down around Middlesboro were bottle-feeding theirs so they wouldn't have to admit that they were mountain girls.

"A couple of weeks after you were born, I happened to run into the doc in the hospital cafeteria. I wasn't scheduled for a checkup yet, but I'd gone over to fill out some insurance forms. He was taking a coffee break, and asked me to have a cup with him. Once we were sitting down, he gave me the eye from top to toe, stirring his coffee with a swizzle stick. 'You're looking pretty healthy, you heifer. You could stand to lose a few pounds, but otherwise I'd say you're in the pink. How you getting along with the feedings? As well-rested as you look, I guess you decided to follow my advice and start the baby on formula right off.' I hiked up my blouse, unhooked the left cup of my nursing bra, and gave him a tableful of milk. When it hit the formica, I felt the letdown. A stream squirted across the table dead into the center of his tie. I looked him in the eye and said, 'You want some cream with that coffee?' That's the last I ever heard about breast feeding."

The two of them laughed together. "I'd give anything to have seen the look on that doctor's face."

"You know we want you to be happy, don't you, baby? That's the most important thing to us."

"I know it. And I'm trying to be. It's not that easy, for me anyway. I can't figure out what I'm doing wrong."

Josie adjusted the gas lantern, lengthening its shadow and theirs across the picnic table. "Do you ever think about having children?"

"I have a hard enough time taking care of myself, much less a baby."

"Of course. I don't mean right away, but down the road. Your father would love to be a grandfather. I believe it would give him something else to live for. And you really have a way with kids. There's a reason why you've worked as a nanny, and in a day-care center."

"Is Dad getting worse? He looks better to me than he did a few months ago."

"He has a few more years left. But no one can say how long. And as much fuss as he puts up, I do know he'd like more than anything else to see you finally settled in your own life. Having a child gives you an anchor. It brings you out of yourself. Before me and Carson ever got together, I had a vision of you, clear as anything, just the way women do nowadays when they look at an ultrasound, your feet and arms and shoulders, all shapely and small and downy, with lanugo around you like a chick, and your perfect little mouth, and even a shock of taffy blonde hair atop your head, more hair than you ever see on a baby, and I could foretell from that vision that Carson and I were going to marry and that I would birth you inside a year. When you were born prematurely, you looked exactly the way my vision said you would. And I believe you have the same kind of second sight in you. You just need a child to bring it out."

She patted Serena on the leg. "I'm happy that you and Robbie have gotten together, doll. He's a good person. Your father will get used to the idea pretty soon too. There was a time when he thought of Robbie as the son he never had, so it's hard for Carson to start thinking about him in another way. But I hope that things will work out between you. I need to go inside and get started on these cakes. If you want to stay out here for a while, I can leave the lantern on, unless you'd prefer to sit in the dark. But once the light's gone, the mosquitos come. We've patched all the holes in the screen, but somehow or other a few get through anyway."

"Turn out the light, please." Serena sat in darkness, feeling the invisible waves of heat. The temperature had scarcely dropped since nightfall, and the air hung heavy with the scent and cling of humidity. She lit a cigarette. Below, beside the landing in the stairs, the violet coil of the bug zapper glowed. The coil incinerated insects continuously, its low-pitched crackle as much a white noise as the crickets, one you didn't hear unless you listened for it or were at the cabin for the first time as a visitor. After a short stay, even visitors forgot about it. It destroyed as many mosquitos as it could, but there were too many of them. The bogs and puddles among the ground cover made a perfect breeding ground. Serena felt a mild itch as a mosquito pricked her arm in the dark. Setting her cigarette on the picnic table, she moved her hand slowly downward until it was poised above her forearm. She gave a quick slap, and the feeding stopped.

II
♒

≈

My carnal life I will lay down
Because it is depravéd
I'm sure on any other ground
I never can be savéd

My heart is filled with toils, and so
I'll seek humiliation
And if I'm true my work to do
I know I'll find salvation

—Shaker hymn

〰 She and Robbie had chosen the upstairs bedroom, the one with the sloping ceiling where the eaves came down. They didn't want Matt and Shar to feel that they'd been shortchanged. So they gave them the master bedroom, which had an iron heating stove in it, with a broad round pipe that disappeared into the ceiling.

The place was even more isolated than she had remembered from her first visit. After they'd finished unpacking the essential items, she went in search of the waterfall, through bramble-choked fields. She kept having to climb barbed-wire fences. No animals were in sight, however. When the four of them had bought the place, they hadn't even thought to ask about livestock. Perhaps the farmer had auctioned them off, or perhaps, as his metabolism slowed down and his memory faded, he had simply stopped feeding and milking the livestock, even forgotten that they existed, now that he bought his bacon in a package. She couldn't bear the thought that the animals might have languished indefinitely, awaiting in a dim and restive way their own impending extinction. Some of the mares could have been carrying foals, but those would have been stillborn on account of the weakness of the mares. The cows would have lowed and lowed, their udders filled to bursting as they waited in vain for the farmer to cross the fields and relieve them. She comforted herself by reasoning that since she hadn't come across any carcasses, the animals had probably been shipped off to auction. As she traversed pasture after pasture, picking up clusters of burrs on her pant legs, moving further and further from the farmhouse, she kept thinking that she would spy at least one lone cow or horse somewhere along the way, but there were none to be had.

She entered a black barn, open at both ends, that made her think of a wayside church of the kind her father might preach in. Implements had been left here and there, leaning against barrels or hung on nails, implements whose uses she hadn't a clue about. They were simply pieces of metal to her, abstract shapes that might as easily have been used for liturgical purposes as for farming. The floor was littered with hay, some of it baled, some of it flung in an irregular carpet. Sitting on one of the bales, she lifted her legs, situated herself, and drank in the silence. Tilting her head, she looked upward into the barn's rafters. Shapes hung in rows that she took to be tobacco drying. She seemed to remember something about that from the visits to her grandparents as a child. They topped the tobacco plants, then hung them up to cure. A draught of fresh wind sluiced through the barn, and the tobacco leaves fluttered ever so slightly.

Peering at the dark outlines, she perceived heads on them, and wings instead of leaves, and it dawned on her that they were bats hanging upside down. Leaping to her feet, she ran crazily in zigzags away from the barn, the way she might have run if she'd discovered a wasp flying around her head. Panting, feeling foolish, she sank to the ground a couple of hundred yards off. Spears of goldenrod reached above her head. The silence of the bats had made her freak. She wondered how long they had hung there, days or weeks or months, whether they were in some sort of hibernation, and what would happen if she hurled a stone up into their midst. Would they scatter into the lofts, swoop down at her head with shrieks, or would struck ones drop to the straw-covered barn floor, like stalactites, inert and mineral?

As she trampled through still more unmown land, she completely lost sight of the farmhouse on the horizon. The movement of her legs and feet sent scads of minute green insects springing out of the grass with every step, and white butterflies circled her waist before fluttering away. The insects gave her solace, as if she had been swimming in a coral reef among schools of tropical fish. She crashed down a steep slope that led to the river.

As she hastened ever downward, a view of the river came into sight. When she burst through the last of the brush, she found herself on a narrow bank of rock and dirt, one just big enough for two people to stand on. Down the bank, on another outcropping of land, a steel cable hung from an immense oak. The cable must have been eighty feet in length, and there were no lower branches on the tree. She couldn't imagine who might have hung the cable, or how they'd managed it. Somebody had used it to swing out far over the river and drop into the water. The Kentucky was muddy, chocolate brown, and didn't appear to be moving very fast. When she had told Robbie she was going out for a hike, he warned her to be careful in case she went down to the river for a swim, because the speed of the flow could be deceptive. A few hundred yards downstream, a bend in the river made it impossible to see any further beyond. Upstream, a wide tributary, its water a clear green, fed into the Kentucky.

As they were unpacking, Robbie had gotten frisky and suggested that they consummate the oak bed and quilt bequeathed to her by Lila. Her mother and grandmother had both been born in the oak bed. She would make it up to Robbie tonight, as best she could. He hadn't put any more pressure on her, just shrugged and gone back to unpacking his clothes.

The more she thought about it, there was every reason in the world for her have a baby by Robbie. Now was as good a time as any. Her father had never said a word directly to her about it, and never would unless she broached the subject first, but she knew it would make him supremely happy. Even though he would raise Cain about its being born out of wedlock, that is, in the event that she and Robbie didn't marry, Carson would, within himself, probably see the birth as Providence's way of putting her life in order, and rejoice in it.

The problem was how to bring the subject up to Robbie. Robbie might feel uptight about her pregnancy at first too, on account of his and her own money situation, and she didn't want to scare him off by pressuring him too soon. But he did have the engineering job, and she sensed that in his heart of hearts he was pining for fatherhood. What if it just happened, spontaneously? He would flee from it as an abstract idea, but welcome it as a fait accompli. Wouldn't she be doing him a favor, in a way, if she let herself get knocked up? And wasn't that her desire too? Wasn't that what moving out to the country was all about? She would have to keep the secret entirely to herself until she began to show, so as not to provoke any outcries from Matt and especially from Shar, who was infertile, and who in any case wasn't having relations with Matt. Maybe the child would bring Shar and her closer together. Shar could be a kind of unofficial aunt, or they might end up raising her together, the four of them.

All she had to do was stop using her diaphragm. Nothing could be simpler. Robbie wasn't the kind who ever thought about things like that. He simply took it for granted that the woman was on some form of birth control, that it was her responsibility, her dilemma. That was part of what fascinated her about him, the fact that he assumed he would pass through life unscathed. However much he might talk about administering CPR to victims of drowning, or not wanting his friends to mourn him should he fall prey to a fatal accident, within himself he believed that he would live forever, just like those seventeen-year-olds he temporized about. Chances were he'd already fathered a child or two, without knowing it, but he possessed the childlike self-assurance that neither illegitimate fatherhood, nor venereal disease, nor locusts nor famine nor anything else would come to trouble his unstinting, boyish lust for life.

If he walked, she would bring it up herself. She didn't flinch from that possibility. She had a sudden desire to take a swim in the river's fast current. Wading through the shallow stagnant water between the roots that stuck out along the eroded bank, she reached the tree. Grasping the steel cable, she walked uphill as far as the length of it would allow. She took a running start down the bank, and with a thrust of her muscular legs, pushed herself out into space. The ground beneath vanished, and the gravity of her body took her first down to where her feet almost skimmed the surface of the water, then upward in a swift arc that whipped her around to where she could see a piece of the river below, brown and solid like an expanse of cement wall. Her hands held fast to the twisted bundle of rusty metal fibers, thick as a high voltage wire, until she swung back to the bank in a rush and dropped onto the wet dirt.

Picking her spattered self up, she rubbed her chapped hands together and placed them on her thighs, panting. She was bent over like a diver who has suffered a dizzy spell and had to walk away from the platform in humiliation. She knew the posture well, because she'd seen it any number of times at competitions. It had never happened to her. Though her technique was far from perfect, she had gained a reputation as someone who never walked away from any dive, and would attempt the most difficult ones. Of all the many things that provoked anxiety in her, water had never been one of them. It was the one element she had mastered, her proving ground, the place where she always felt comfortable, no matter the circumstances.

The sun had lowered behind the treetops on the opposite bank. She'd promised Robbie and the others she wouldn't be away overly long, that she would take responsibility for driving into town, buying groceries, and preparing their first supper, since the three of them had agreed to keep unpacking while she took her walk. If she lingered much longer, Robbie would come looking for her.

Amber light slanted across the fields, making it hard to retrace her route, but she knew that she had travelled roughly east away from the farmhouse. She faced directly into the setting sun and climbed the fences of the pastures, trying not to pierce her skin on barbs as strands of fence gave way under her weight the way a high wire gives under an acrobat. A twilight haze hung over the grass of the empty fields. She had to keep staring directly into the sun in order to stay oriented westward. In a peculiar way, she felt a compulsion to stare directly into its center, not caring whether it might damage her eyes. If the sun had been in partial eclipse, it would have made her pleasure even keener. It was hard to know how close or far away she was from anything.

She clambered over a fence of wooden slats and found herself standing ankle deep in the mud of a pigsty. Off to her left, she heard a low, inarticulate noise that gradually distinguished itself as grunting. Turning away from the sun, she could make out a sow, detached from its background, the first animal she'd seen on the grounds. The sow of her nightmare. A welter of squeals came from piglets heaped in a far corner of the sty. The teats of the sow were full and heavy, reaching halfway to the ground. Dropping to her hands and knees, Serena crawled slowly toward the sow through the mud. The sow gave her a deliberate, dubious look, and its litany of grunts deepened, but it didn't back away from her approach. They stayed like that for a long moment, taking each other's measure, until Serena let her torso slide down to where she could wallow in the loam. Over and over she turned, letting the mud work its way into her hair, her clothes, the crevices of her knees and neck. On her feet again, she registered the barnyard around her and the weathered house with its windows prematurely and uncannily illuminated for evening.

" My God, what happened to you?"
"It's nothing. I tripped and fell coming over a fence."
"You're filthy. It's all in your hair and everyplace."
"I know. It was slippery, so I had to wallow to get back on my feet. I'll run out for groceries as soon as I have a chance to shower and change my clothes."
"I already went," said Shar. "We couldn't wait any longer, so I drove to a little store down the road to pick up a few things. They were about to close, so I got lucky. I cooked porkchops and mashed potatoes. There's some left for you under the plate over there on the counter."
"Porkchops? Actually, the thought of pork makes me queasy right now. But thanks for making them, and taking my turn," she hastened to add. "I'm sure they're delicious. I got lost on my hike. I'll clean up the dishes, and do a full shopping tomorrow."
"Suit yourself. Don't tell me you're a vegetarian, and we're going to have to cook special meals for you."
"It's not that. I just can't eat when I'm getting adjusted to a new place. Too much excitement, I guess."
"Man," said Matt, "I wish we had some animals of our own,

then we could go slaughter one whenever we needed to, and cure our own meat. Have ribs or sausage anytime. I bet Robbie could dress a hog, couldn't you, hoss? He can debone and filet fish faster than anybody I ever saw. We should have bargained with that old dude to leave us some livestock."

"We do have a hog. And its babies. I found them in a pen out beyond the first pasture."

Matt clapped his hands. "Hot dog. Or hot hog, I guess I should say. We can fatten them up for winter. I was looking around and there's a beautiful smokehouse. We might as well make use of it."

"I don't think we should kill them."

"Why not, babe?" Robbie sat atop the counter in jeans, shirt off and a sweatband around his head. "Pigs don't serve any other purpose in this life except makin' bacon. You don't have religious objections, do you?"

"No, actually I'm becoming a witch."

"I see. Like Circe. So maybe that hog is one of your past boyfriends who got out of line." He had a slight smirk on his face.

"No, the hog is a she, a sow. That's how she was able to have piglets."

"Oh, well, maybe you got pissed at one of my old girlfriends, then."

"If we've got meat, I don't see any reason why we shouldn't use it. We need to cut corners any way we can," said Shar. "You wouldn't believe how much I had to pay for those porkchops. Tomorrow, the four of us are going to sit down and draw up a budget for this month's expenses, so we'll know how much income we have to work with, and what our expenditures are going to be."

"I'm glad we have a business head in the house," said Robbie. "I took all kinds of calculus, but when it comes to budgets, I can't make the numbers add up right."

"You know, honey, maybe we should all become vegetarians," Matt offered. "I mean it. When you don't eat fatty meat, your health risks for, well, you know, a lot of things go down."

She gave him a warning look. "Let's not get on that subject, please. I know how to take care of myself."

"At least let me take responsibility for feeding and raising the pigs," said Serena. "When winter comes, we can decide what to do about them."

"Suits me fine," said Shar, unwrapping a serving bowl from a wrinkled sheet of the funny papers. The dark circles under Shar's eyes were more prominent than usual. She seemed less combative than worn down. Her expression said that she wanted to like people, even love them, if she could only remember how to be happy and out of pain.

"I'm really happy we all went in on this buy together," Serena said to her. "It might be the best thing that ever happened to us."

"It might," Shar answered with a hopeless sigh. "Where do you want this clock, in the kitchen or in your room?"

That night in the iron bed, Serena was passionate with Robbie. She told him to lie back and let her do the work. He didn't seem to mind obeying that instruction. Propped on a pillow, he lay with his arms crossed behind his head. He wore an easygoing smile, the kind that came naturally to him, while he watched her labor. She sat astride him, her arms propped on his chest. By her rough calculations, she had ovulated about two days ago, maybe a little less. She was grateful she'd gone off the pill a couple of years before, when she'd grown tired of an unrewarding string of men.

"Serena baby, you're like a woman on a mission. I'm glad you went out on that walk today. Whatever it was, it sure changed your mood."

She brought her body down closer to his. "It's because I'm ready now."

"You were always a little bit wild and crazy, doing pranks and stuff, but I never pictured what you'd be like in bed. I had to get over that thing about us growing up together."

She was licking at his ear now, breathing into it, whispering, trying to make the hair on his neck tingle. "Treat me the way you would one of your campfire girls. I'm a bad girl. That night in the car, I couldn't wait to get my mouth around it."

"Oh, God." He wrapped his arms around her, groaning, and pulled her to him with an almost crushing force. He came at once, in a single spasm. She came too, but in a different way, with a melting and entirely inward sweetness. When they uncoupled, she rolled over, propped her feet on the footboard at once and lay on her back with a pillow beneath her legs so nothing would spill out of her. He sat on the side of the bed, looking around in vain for something to do, to read, something to occupy his hands. But there was nothing in the room except cardboard boxes and a couple of lamps without bulbs in them.

"Maybe I should do a little unpacking before we turn the light out."

"Come to bed."

"I'm not very sleepy."

"Are you disappointed? I thought you preferred it like that. I can be more wifey next time, if that's more comfortable for you."

"I do like it, kind of. A lot, actually. But when it's over, I can't deal with it."

"You worry too much. I'm the one who grew up in a Baptist household, not you."

"That's just it. Me knowing your folks so well. Sooner or later, I'm going to have to go over there for dinner, and we'll start talking over old times. It's too weird. We'll probably have to go to church with them." He turned to face her. "I don't want them to think I'm avoiding them, because I really like your dad. Your mom too. Do you think we should get married or something? He can perform the ceremony and then we can all totally max out on the weirdness of the situation."

"I'm not in any hurry. There will be plenty of time for that, if you decide in a few months that's what you still want. You don't have to worry about my folks. I've already talked everything over with them, and they've accepted it."

"If you say so. I don't know how to put this, but could we try to be more, like, normal with each other? There's something not quite healthy about the way we're relating. Maybe we should go canoeing."

"I want to be normal," she answered dreamily, her eyes shut. "More than anything in the world. I'm starting to feel more normal all the time. For the first time in my life, I'm really happy. Could you hand me some toilet paper? I think there's a roll in that box over by the wall."

He handed it to her and snuggled up beside her, pulling the sheet over both of them. Ever so gently, he stroked her forehead, as if she had a fever he wanted to soothe. "I love you, Serena," he whispered. "You believe me, don't you?"

"I love you too." They lay in blissful silence, listening to the whir of the ceiling fan. "Robbie?"

"Yeah, babe."

"Why is it that guys enjoy that kind of talk so much?"

"I don't know, man. I guess we're just sick or something."

The owner of the canoe rental shop down in the Gorge gestured to the wooden racks of inverted canoes outside, red and green, numbers stamped on the end in white, and told them to take their pick. Business had been slow, because the level of the river was unusually low for this time of year. They could see for themselves by looking at the water mark when they passed underneath the first bridge. That made for a lot more shoals, and most of the people who came from close around, in the county, wanted a nice, easy ride; in fact, he rented more rubber innertubes than he did canoes, because what they liked more than anything was to pop an Ale-Eight and drift down lazy and slow, talking to each other while the innertubes bumped together. The only sporty ones were the fishermen, and they usually had their own rigs. It just hadn't been a real good year for business. At least they hadn't dammed up the Red River like they had the Kentucky; then the speedboats would come down and overrun the place. Did they know how to paddle through white water? It wasn't that difficult really, but he'd be happy to run over the basics with them, because the current seemed a bit fast today.

"That's okay," said Robbie. "I've run this river before, and so has he."

"Do you folks want life jackets or flotation cushions?"

"We don't need those," said Matt. "All of us know how to swim. Those two even know all about lifeguarding and CPR." He pointed at Serena and Robbie. "And I've got enough body fat, I'll float anyway."

"Flotation devices are required by law," the old man answered. "I ain't got no liability insurance neither. Can't afford it."

"Nobody's going out on the river with me who doesn't have a life preserver," said Robbie. "The ones who think it won't happen to them are always the ones who end up having something happen. You know that, Matt."

"You sound like a public service announcement, dude."

"I'm glad one of you has some sense. Which will it be?"

"She and I will take life jackets."

"Same for me," said Shar. "If you have one my size."

"Give me a cushion," said Matt. "At least it will protect my butt from that hard aluminum seat. Those are worse than church pews. They ought to give us little cardboard fans along with the life preservers."

When they had slid the canoes over the dirt and down into the water, Robbie reached out a paddle for each of the other three to hold onto until they had found their feet in the rocking canoes. The two women sat in front, the men in back. Shoving off, they drifted downstream, paddling easily, splitting to either side of the bridge support. On it, a handpainted water mark showed the river to be five feet down.

"Not bad," said Robbie. "A little low, but not full fathom five. I was expecting more, from the look of things. This is an easy river. The roughest water we should run into is a class two." Serena slung one leg over the seat, to watch him scan the water ahead, the bank, reading it, making sense of it all. It made her feel easy in her mind to be taken care of this way, to entrust herself to someone knowledgeable and loving. "You still remember how to do this, dude?" Robbie called out to the other canoe. "It's been a long time since we came down here together."

"I think it'll come back. Since I was always strung out when I canoed before, I ought to handle it even better now. Remember the little stand over in Nada where they made milkshakes in a huge tin canister? The guy would drop in a big gob of peanut butter, a banana, some chocolate ice cream, and let it rip in the mixer. Bo*da*cious."

"Ooh, don't even get me started. Maybe we can stop in there on the way back." Robbie participated in the patter appropriately but absently. His mind seemed to have entered into its own space, but one that also included her. "You comfortable up there, babe?"

"I'm fine."

"I don't know how it is you and me never were on the water together, as much camping as we all did down here. Pay attention to what's going on upstream of a rock, and see how the water splits around it. That shows you which way the current is going to flow, and where the eddies lie. See how it makes a V? This is a lot easier than learning the constellations, because the rocks are all doing pretty much the same thing. Still, you have to take a bunch of them in at one time. We're coming up on a little shoal, a class one. This will be good practice. Now, we're going to maneuver it towards the middle, first right and then real quick to the left again. Okay, put your paddle down in the water on the left side. Paddle hard." She dipped hers into the water and gave a few lackadaisical strokes. "Come on, Serena, get down on it." When they had negotiated the shoal, she turned around and saw the peeved look on his face. "That was pretty halfassed. If this had been a class three or four, we would have landed in deep shit."

She laughed. "You don't have to get so ticked. I thought you were in control. You're the one steering us, right? Didn't you say you only pretended to your river rafters that they had some control so they'd feel they were getting their money's worth?"

"It's different in a big rubber raft. Even then, they have to cooperate if they don't want to flip. They can't help that much, it's true, but they can sure screw things up if they want to. Here, it's two people in an aluminum canoe. I steer, yeah, but if you don't do your part, we both end up in the drink. So when I shout instructions, listen."

"Aye, aye, cap'n. I'll try to be a good first mate."

"Okay." His face was so uncharacteristically serious, she wanted to hug him. They had entered another stretch of easy water, the only sound the plash of their paddles, regular and soft. The trees along the shore grew just far enough apart that she could glimpse between them into the uneven corridors speckled with light. Shar and Matt had coasted ahead. Both of them looked as content as she'd ever seen them. Matt was pointing out a log that had made an impromptu dam. Shar sat with her paddle across her lap while Matt took care of the necessary strokes. Any time the canoe slowed, he gave several heaves, like an oarsman. He was offering his physical strength to Shar like a gift, and today, she seemed willing, even eager, to receive it. Her face, from a distance anyway, had lost its pallor, and her lank black hair fell in a becoming, almost maidenly fashion behind her ears. A sparkle shone through in her expression.

Another run of mild shoals came up, and Robbie called out for her to paddle hard left, harder, then stop, wait, wait, then again, again, again, okay stop good job babe. In the next few sets of shoals, she followed his instructions, and started to perceive the logic of the current. Matt's style of talking Shar through each run was different from Robbie's altogether. Matt coaxed her, his voice forgiving and gentle.

The difference in styles didn't really bother her. She understood that Robbie expected his woman to be capable, that he would teach her everything she needed to know about the wilderness, but that he would also take it for granted that she would be able to learn what he taught within a reasonable amount of time. If they had been hiking on the Appalachian Trail, and her strength began to give out, say, half a mile before the designated stopping point for the day, she wondered whether he would slow down to walk at her pace, or whether he would go on ahead, telling her that he was going to reach the shelter and start setting up camp.

"Did you ever hike on the Appalachian Trail?"

"Yeah, a few times. I did a stretch in North Carolina with a couple of guys I knew. I was hiking first, the other two guys behind me, and it was getting toward sunset. Visibility wasn't that great, so we're going along not saying anything and it's real quiet, so I'm spacing out, you know. I look down and I'm about to step on a rattlesnake coiled up smack in the middle of the path. Half a step more and I would have put my foot right in the center of him. Freaked me out. I started backpedaling. That sucker raised its head up, rattle started shaking fast. I thought sure it was going to strike. If it had, I would have been s. o. l., because in those days I never thought to carry a snakebite kit, first aid, nothing like that. There's no way they could have gotten me medical attention in time. But it didn't strike. I guess it just wasn't my time. After that, those guys called me the snake charmer."

"Are you saying you think Providence was protecting you?"

"I don't know what to call it. Isis."

"I'm serious. What do you think it is? God?"

He thought a minute. "Placebo effect. But if it works, I'm not knocking it."

"I had a feeling you were going to say something like that."

A curtain of water came raining over the side of the canoe. "Hey, what the hell?"

Matt's deep laugh sounded close by. "Got you, fucker." He'd pulled the canoe close to theirs, and sent spray flying with his paddle.

"This is war, buddy. Nobody soaks the river king and lives to tell about it." Robbie and Matt went at it, paddles dishing water, screeching like two wildmen. Serena joined in, then Shar, shouting and laughing.

"Get them! Get them!"

"Hey, what are you doing? We're in the same boat. Traitor."

"Wait, I dropped my paddle. Truce, truce."

Drenched, arms hanging limp, they rested, letting the canoes drift until they clacked together. "That cooled me down. I didn't realize how hot it was getting. God, this is the life." The sun had risen fully over them, and the river broadened. A long shelf of limestone rose up on the eastern side, and by coming in close to it, they were afforded a shady spot. They unwrapped pimiento cheese sandwiches and dug in. "This tastes incredibly good," Robbie said with his mouth full. "Course, when Matt's royalties start pouring in, we can have fresh salmon flown out to the farm for our picnics. Or maybe we'll just stock the pond with salmon, have some experts from the agriculture school at UK come out and create a little ecosystem."

"Here's a beer for everybody too," said Matt. "Yeah, I talked to the Nashville guy a couple of days ago, and he said George Strait had asked to look at it. Could be a hit. Remember the time we all got lost down a blind alley here in the Gorge? Nothing around but cliffs, and we bushwhacked up a really long hill. I tell you, hot KoolAid in a plastic canteen never tasted so good."

"Yeah, that was one of Robbie's famous shortcuts."

"Don't lay it on me. I told you guys I'd meet you back at the car if you didn't want to explore with me. I take one shortcut in my whole life, and I have to hear about it for years afterward." The other three burst out laughing.

"Right, one shortcut. If you're walking along and a sign says Danger, the one thing you can be sure of is that Robbie will head straight for it," said Shar. Watching her mobile, animated face, Serena could remember what she'd been like in high school, before the grimness set in.

"What can I say? It's in my genes. Can you believe, it's been fifteen years since the four of us were together on an outing? It's as though nothing had changed during all that time." No one contradicted him. They sat for a long while in silence, reverently sectioning their oranges, as though a single word spoken would shatter the fragility of the moment. When lunch was over, they glided away from the limestone cliff, one canoe following the other. Past the next bend, the water turned shallower and faster. Its passage among the protruding rocks made a sizeable and visible flume. It was their first real rapids. Robbie turned the canoe sideways and kept it almost motionless with flicks of his paddle, as did Matt.

"This flow is faster than what I thought we'd find. It's about a class three. You sure you can shoot this one, Matt?"

"You're not talking to one of your Denver computer programmers. I grew up knowing the Red River. When I get to the bottom of this run, I'm going to make you kiss my hairy ass. Me and Shar are a good little team. You two just sit back and watch the pros go to work. Ready, hon?" She nodded, her face sparkling with droplets. Their canoe entered the flume and right away picked up speed. Both of them kept shifting their strokes from one side to the other, as fast as they could, scraping against submerged stones, and Shar fended off a couple of big nasty rocks with the tip of her paddle. The back of the canoe fishtailed, caught, hung still for a moment, until Matt, with a tremendous thrust, righted it. The last of the flume dumped them into the tranquil water at the bottom, where the canoe skidded sideways in slow motion until they both were visible to the canoe at the top. Matt gave Robbie an exaggerated, provocative wave, a victory wave, one that clearly said, Come on down, if you can, the water's fine.

"All right, Serena. The flow is going to pull us to the left. See the way it shoots off the big shelf just ahead of us? All I want you to do is pull as hard as you can to the right, with all your strength, and if we do happen to get hung on a rock, push against the river bed. If you do your part, I'll take care of the rest. There's a shallow spot about halfway down that they squeaked through by sheer luck. They hit it exactly right. Matt's pretty good, but he probably doesn't even realize how tricky that could have been if his canoe had been turned a hair. It would have thrown them out and, with him not wearing a life vest, who knows what might have happened."

"I'm glad you told me that. Now I'm nervous."

"Nothing to be nervous about, babe. Just do what I said and we'll have it covered. There's not going to be any time for me to talk or pay attention to what you're doing. That's why I'm going over it."

Serena drew a big breath. "Okay." She turned to give him one last look. "Do I really have any control, sitting here up front?"

He smiled back. "What do you think?" He veered their canoe into the flume, and it hurtled downriver. The speed was much greater than she would have imagined, even from watching Matt and Shar go through. Looking down into the frothing stream, she hacked at the water. For an instant, she thought she could feel the bottom of the canoe catch, barely hesitate, then it was drawn down into the thickest part of the flume, which nearly enveloped them. The canoe seemed airborne for an instant, spray arcing up all around, then she looked up and their canoe was in easy water, pulling alongside the other one. Matt gave her a thumbs up. She had no idea whether her exertions had actually made a difference, or whether Robbie had managed their descent all by himself. If she asked him, of course he would tell her she'd been an equal partner in it, but she wasn't so sure. It had happened so quickly, virtually without a hitch, that she'd had no time to process what was happening except the giddy feeling of being sucked to the bottom of the flume by the water's force.

"Okay, showoff. You win points for technique. Not a flaw in your performance. But me and Shar went down on sheer balls. We're the trailblazers."

"My hat's off to you, O pioneers."

"Anyway, Serena was the brains of your operation. All you could provide was brute force, and the way that stream was cooking along, you didn't need any force."

"I can't deny it. I was just in the back seat." They all surveyed the cascade behind them. "God damn. I'm starting to think that was a class four, now that I get a good look at it. That spout is raging. It's a beauty. Good thing we were flying blind." Robbie slithered over the side, calf deep in the shallows, and pulled the canoe to a secure resting place. "I don't know if you guys would mind waiting, but I'd like to shoot that rapid with my body."

"What the hell are you talking about, man? We barely got through there in our canoes. You can't bodysurf that rapid."

"Right. No way," said Serena.

Already, Robbie was clambering over dry boulders, picking his way upward. "You guys relax. I've done this kind of thing at least a hundred times. I'll be down in a matter of seconds. The way the water makes a chute, it should actually be easier with something smaller like my body than with a big clunky canoe. It's a matter of getting myself into the stream without slipping on wet rocks. I have my vest on, which is more than I can say for some people."

"I'm serious," said Matt with unaccustomed heat. "We don't need your thrill-seeking right now. You've never shot a rapid that size with your body. Let's not push our luck."

Robbie gave them one last smile. Serena knew him too well from all the years they'd spent as friends. He wasn't one to get into protracted arguments. He simply did what he'd decided in the first place, regardless of what others thought or said.

Matt started to go after him, but she put her hand on his shoulder.

"I'm not letting him do that. He'll kill himself."

"If that's what he has to do, then that's what he has to do." She knew that the climb was too precarious for Matt, and anyway, he wouldn't be able to move fast enough to catch Robbie. With his long extremities, Robbie was a natural climber, and it didn't take him long to find his way up. He disappeared behind a boulder near the top, then came out the other side. His body moved with the total confidence of someone who has always landed on his feet. The snake charmer. Shaking his newly grown bangs out of his face, he sidled into the water. From the gingerly way he crept, she could tell that the surface was very slick. But he didn't tense up. In his ability to relax and let his body go limp, he was like a child. One of the children she'd sat for as a nanny, a two-year-old, had fallen backward down the stairs one time, before she could reach out to catch him, and when she ran down to help him up, he didn't have a scratch on him.

When Robbie reached the middle of the stream, he sat down and positioned himself. He obviously had found something to anchor him. She had no doubt he was smiling. For an instant, he looked like he could have been sitting in a sleepy little creek, bathing. Then he brought his feet up, raised his legs slightly out of the water, and his slender body was propelled into the channel. Water rushed over him, revealing only parts of his torso and face. He resembled a being emerging from a moving shroud, pulsing with vital force. He had calculated almost perfectly how the currents would carry him, because it looked for sure as if he would come all the way to the bottom in a single fluid motion. About halfway down, there was a slight hesitation, almost imperceptible. Robbie's body pitched out of the stream, rolled over several shoals, jerking from the contact, and was dumped into the pool.

For a moment, she remained looking back up toward where he had sat before he let go, as if she expected that to give her some clue as to what had happened. He was no longer there, she knew, but she still had to be sure, and her eye retraced the path of his descent. The way he thrashed in the pool below, she could see he was hurt, but at least he was conscious. She scrambled over the side of the canoe before the others could react. Trying not to get herself too agitated, she swam to him with deliberate strokes. The fact that he had on a life preserver gave her time. Getting behind him, she wrapped one arm around his limp body and frog-kicked her way to the side. With an effort, and with his feeble help, she was able to push him onto shore. He had gashes on his chest, arms, and face. A fair amount of blood was coming from one of the chest gashes, and she started to apply pressure to it, but he lifted his head and shook it in violent disagreement, saying, "My leg, it's my leg that hurts." When she surveyed it, nothing seemed to be bruised, then she saw the dislocation of his knee, shoved far out of its socket, and knew there was going to be plenty of torn cartilage. From the look of vacant disbelief he gave her, she thought he might well be in shock. A hideous misunderstanding had taken place. He had a contract with the universe, and injury wasn't a part of it. "Lie still," she said to him, as calmly as she could, "and breathe into the cup of my hand. That's good." She knew that she might have to pay later for any lies she told now, but it didn't matter. "Everything is going to be perfectly fine," she said. "In a month's time you'll be right back out here on the river."

"Can I get you anything before I go out to weed the herb garden?"

Robbie's splinted leg was elevated on a stack of pillows, under an ice pack, the flesh still yellowish brown around the kneecap. The cuts on his torso and arms had scabbed over. He was reading a Tom Robbins novel, and he didn't look up. "Nah, I guess I'm okay."

"More Coke?"

"Not unless you mean cocaine."

"If you think of anything, the window's open, and I'm just outside, okay?"

"Sure."

Serena sat on the edge of the bed. She was half tempted to snatch the book out of his hands. She'd bought it for him to read during his overnight hospital stay, and she understood that his absorption in it was at first his way of not admitting that he was in a hospital, but he hadn't put the book down since she and Matt and Shar had gotten him situated in the bed. He must have read it three times already. Because he couldn't go up and down stairs, and to make it easier for her to see to his needs, Shar and Matt had given them the downstairs room, after some heated discussion behind closed doors, which she pretended not to have noticed. She and Robbie were sleeping in Shar's brass bed, and the four of them had had to switch all of their clothes and personal belongings only days after they'd gotten settled. Serena would have done almost anything to avoid taking their room away so soon, but there was no upstairs bathroom, and even though this was an old farmhouse, she didn't think a chamberpot would be very practical under the circumstances. So, she'd agreed to accept their generosity. "You'll mend," she said, giving his good leg a gentle stroke.

She could hear him exhaling air through his nostrils. "Go ahead and tell me," he said, from behind the pages.

"Tell you what?"

At last, he set the book down on his lacerated chest. "Tell me I'm a fool. Tell me I shouldn't have attempted that run, and that all of you tried to talk me out of it, but I wouldn't listen."

"Why do I need to say anything? Anyway, it doesn't make any difference. It happened, and it's done. Nobody wants to say I told you so. The only question now is how we deal with the consequences."

"At least I've been at my job a month, so I qualify for health insurance. There's a two-fifty deductible, but they'll pick up the rest. I wish we weren't way the hell out here, an hour-and-fifteen-minute commute from my job. If we lived in Lexington and it was down the road, or even across town, I could get back to work a lot sooner."

She took a couple of deep breaths before answering. "I'm in the same situation, as far as the commute is concerned. I hate to say this, but it wasn't my idea to buy the farm. You agreed to it before I did. All we can do is make the best of a bad situation. Try to forget about it for now. Fretting won't make you heal any faster."

He set the book down beside him and rubbed his face. "Yeah, I know. What in the hell was I thinking when I did that? God, I can't stand being on bedrest. Here I am spending the whole day in bed and we can't even do anything."

"Your leg doesn't need to be jostled."

He tried to smile, but it came out as a grimace. "How about a blow job?"

"Robbie, please. I need to weed the garden, and then I have to help Shar get dinner together. Don't forget, the three of us are having to take up the slack. We don't mind, but it has to be done all the same."

"Right. With these pain killers I'm on, I probably couldn't get it up anyway." He sighed and picked the novel back up. "Man, I never realized Tom Robbins was such a shitty writer. I used to like his stuff. These fucking metaphors go on for half a page at a time. I wish I'd brought some Isaac Asimov along."

In the kitchen, Shar sat at the table peeling potatoes on a sheet of newspaper with a paring knife. Her movements were unusually swift, and Serena seemed to remember that she used to volunteer in a soup kitchen. "How's Johnny Weismuller?"

"Maudlin. He can't stand to be confined."

"I hate to bring this up, when Robbie's just started to convalesce, but our next mortgage payment is due in two weeks. Does he qualify for disability, sick leave, something like that?"

Serena hated to be put in this position. Each of them had agreed to be responsible individually for their part of the mortgage payment, but Shar for practical purposes considered her and Robbie a unit. "He's applied, but it doesn't look good. He hasn't been there long enough. If it had happened on the job, workman's comp would have picked it up."

"Yes, except that I doubt they would have sent him over a waterfall as part of his job description."

"All four of us took a chance going rafting on those rapids, okay? Any of us could have wiped out in our canoes."

"Except we didn't."

"We will meet our obligations. The rent money will be there, one way or another, on the day it's due. You don't need to worry yourself about it."

"Fine. I don't like to be put into the postion of enforcer. I'd much rather spend my time thinking about my own affairs. But the fact is, we signed a hundred and forty thousand dollar contract on this house, of which we've paid only eight thousand, and that farmer is not going to be happy about our payments being late right off."

"The loan officer seemed like a nice guy. Maybe if we tell him what happened, he'll understand and give us an extension."

"Don't count on it. People can always be nice to each other until it comes to money."

"All right, I said the payment will be there, and it will. I don't want to talk about it any more." She gave the screen door a deliberate bang behind her.

Outside, Matt, in shirtsleeves, stared into the bowels of a galvanized washtub he was scouring out. He was doing some pretending of his own. More than anything in the world, he hated conflict. When others fought within his earshot, he felt it as keenly as if he had been involved directly. He was probably blaming himself at the moment for having suggested the idea of their buying a farm together, and especially for the recommendation that they only take a ten-year mortgage. "I found this washtub out in the yard," he said. "It's perfectly good. All it needs is some cleaning up. This would probably cost fifteen dollars at the hardware store."

"You're doing a good job on it," she said, spending on him what little encouragement she had left. "It will save us some money."

He stood up and gave it a dubious kick. "I don't know. Maybe we can store feed in it for the hogs. They're sure not going to be able to live off our table scraps."

Serena knelt in the dirt, put on her gloves, and pulled weeds by hand. Her two cats trotted over and rubbed around her legs, purring.

"Hey, by the way," said Matt. "Did you notice I finished chopping those last few rows of dirt, so you can plant something there now if you want to, autumn stuff like cauliflower, or whatever."

"Thanks. I really appreciate that."

"Yeah," said Matt, standing upright with a frayed scouring pad in his hand. "Only problem is, while I was trying to chop out some of those tough weeds, a big rattlesnake came slithering up through the weed patch and bit my hoe handle."

"Is that so? Must have been the same rattlesnake that almost bit Robbie on the Appalachian Trail. It sure seems to get around."

"It might be. When it bit the hoe, the handle swelled up, and swelled up, and finally got so big I couldn't drag it any more, so I rolled it down the hill, and the hoe made a big new path to the river. We'll be able to drive down now, and have a loading ramp for a boat."

"I'm glad you got some good for all your trouble."

"That's not all. It kept swelling, so I decided to take it down to that sawmill past the county line, the one we always pass on the way to work. They sawed it into lumber, so I brought the lumber back here and built you a new pen for your hogs. But before you thank me, I have some bad news to tell you. Right after I put the hogs in there, the swelling started to go out of the wood, and it shrank down and choked all your hogs to death."

"Hm. I guess there won't be any meat for the smokehouse after all." On her knees, she worked her way along the first bed. The basil, oregano, chamomile, and thyme were already beginning to establish themselves in the garden. The coriopsis and petunias were also thriving. She'd planted watermelon, broccoli, cabbage, tomatoes, zucchini, hot peppers, and rhubarb, but that was all she'd been able to get to so far. She knew she was a good gardener, and could have had the entire huge patch Matt had tilled for her cultivated in only a few days, if she only had enough time available. It was becoming clear that that time was not going to be there, the way things were shaping up. Their idea had been to become as self-subsistent as possible as far as fruits, herbs, and vegetables were concerned. There was no reason they shouldn't be able to do it. She had even learned how to can from Lila and her mother, and had intended to teach Shar so that they could put up beans and tomatoes for the winter.

Now, they were probably going to have to keep running to the little store down the rural route, where they were charged twice as much for everything as they would have had to pay in Lexington. It was ridiculous that there wasn't a farmer's market somewhere close by, but most of the people who lived around there apparently planted only enough in their gardens for themselves, and put the rest of the land into tobacco, corn, or soybeans. Sure, there were trucks here and there that she'd passed by on the way to work, where you could buy corn, or melon, or tomatoes, or some other individual item for cheap, but she would have had to spend all her time, the time she didn't have in the first place, driving the backroads trying to pick up their produce piecemeal. Here they were in the middle of the country, and they had to buy dried-up cucumbers at the store for sixty cents each.

She would ask Stefano tomorrow if he might be able to up her hours at the day-care center. He'd only been able to start her at half time, but had made it clear that once she got broken in to their method, he would up her hours as much as he could, depending on the enrollment. Stefano and his wife had gone over to Italy for a year to study with the founders of the method, and they were very particular about the way that the children be taught. Serena was more accustomed to acting intuitively, using her native skills to relate to children, without a predetermined agenda for the day, and so she felt as if she were going to school at the same time she was teaching it. Stefano was patient and understanding, and always spoke in a soft voice, whether he was talking to a child or an adult, and she and he had even dated briefly in high school, but she always felt that he was watching how she interacted with the children, evaluating her every second. His wife, who took care of the administrative end of things, had spent a fair amount of time walking around writing notes into a chart. That made Serena even more nervous, but Stefano, noticing her jitters, had told her the charting had nothing to do with her, that with all the accusations of sexual harrasment flying around day-care centers these days, they wanted to document as much of the typical activity as they could, to protect themselves.

She hoped, under the circumstances, she would be able to get something approaching full time, even if it meant postponing some of her plans for the farm, most of them probably until next year, because she was going to have to meet Robbie's payments as well as hers until he could convalesce and see whether or not they would retain him at the engineering firm. They liked him all right, but they couldn't wait around indefinitely because they were working on a big cost-plus contract and were stretched about as thin as they could manage, so they'd just have to see what happened. Robbie's parents had made it clear that they didn't want to have anything to do with the whole affair, it was his money and he could do what he wanted with it, but they thought buying the farm was a bad idea and they didn't want him to come running to them later for money, as he inevitably would, after they'd put him through engineering school and he'd gone off and spent the last few years river rafting instead of building a career.

They were glad he had come back to Lexington and started back into his profession; despite all the time and seniority he'd lost, he probably would have been making seventy thousand dollars a year by now if he'd stuck with it, but if he was smart, he'd invest in a condominium in town, something he could make payments on with assurance, instead of going in on an ill-conceived scheme with three other people of varying degrees of dependability. There was no way of telling when one of them might leave him in the lurch, and he'd end up having to cover their mortgage payments as well as his own; they didn't necessarily mean Serena but it was true from what they'd heard that over the years she'd had a hard time holding down a job for very long. His parents weren't likely to loan him any emergency money, especially since he had no intention of telling them what had happened to him on the river; he wasn't going to grovel or give them any opportunity to rub his face in it. Serena would have to make up the difference herself.

She would also have to figure out how to squeeze in the time to take Carson to some of his appointments. The fact that her parents lived out on Chalk Lake, and she down by the river, sixty miles away, and her work was in Lexington, seventy miles away in a different direction, and her father's appointments were in Mt. Sterling, fifteen miles from where he lived, meant that she would have to cover hundreds of miles every week in order to fulfill her obligations. Her parents didn't really expect her to be available, but she had promised her mother; she wanted to do it, to show them that she was responsible and could be counted on in a crisis. Her father had spent years running her and Kelsey to children's theater rehearsals, to ballet and orchestra rehearsals, to dentist and doctor appointments, he alone since her mother didn't drive, and he was often so tired that he would simply park the car and fall asleep in the driver's seat for the length of the rehearsal rather than try to drive home and then have to turn around and come right back. At least that way he could make up piecemeal for some of his lost sleep.

Now that he was in need, she wanted to return the favor. She and Kelsey had been living in New York when he was diagnosed, out of reach except by phone or mail, and now that she was finally in a position to do him some good, she wasn't going to let the opportunity pass.

For now, she was going to have to nurse Robbie, because even though they hadn't been together for long, and weren't married, she liked to think of herself as a devoted person, not one who was just in it for the sex, especially since it looked like there wasn't going to be any sex for a while, and she took seriously the "in sickness and in health" part of things, in spite of the fact that they hadn't taken any vows, or even discussed what they imagined their obligations to one another to be. They hadn't really thought any of that out beforehand, but she liked to think that if the positions were reversed, and she were sick, he would do the same for her, would treat her with tenderness and loving-kindness and nurse her back to health. She wasn't actually so sure that he would, but she was going to go under that assumption until he proved otherwise. Her period was also late, and that was all the more reason she needed to help hasten his healing.

But as soon as she had worked enough extra hours to cover the mortgage, and gotten Robbie back on his feet, and tended to the minimal obligations around the farm—and assuming that the second-hand car which her father had helped her buy held up under the considerable driving strain she was putting it under, since Robbie wouldn't be able to repair it in his current condition, and Matt didn't know the first thing about cars, and neither did her father, even if he'd been well enough to work on it, which he wasn't—but assuming that the car did miraculously hold up, as soon as she had fulfilled her round of tasks, the first thing she planned to do was help drive her father to his doctor appointments in Mount Sterling. Because in the shape he was in he had no business working himself into a state of exhaustion by tending to his pastoral duties and running errands for her mother, and on top of all that getting himself to and from the doctor twice a week. He had a tendency to overwork himself, to try to do too many things at the same time, which was why he'd never been able to tend to his health in the first place, and she wasn't about to let him do that to himself.

Matt knelt beside her and began pulling weeds. "I thought I'd come over and help you out, instead of trying to get that washtub any cleaner. I guess gardening helps you unwind?"

"I'm sorry we can't give you more. If you'll hang on with us until next semester, I can guarantee you full-time work. Guarantee it. The kids love you. By January, I can have you up to thirty-five hours, maybe forty."

"But I need it now."

"I don't know what else to do."

"It's okay. I understand. I figured I didn't have anything to lose by asking."

"If you need a couple hundred bucks, I can loan it to you. You pay it back when you can." At the time she and Stefano dated, it would have been hard for her to imagine him running a child-care center. He played football, and used to get belligerently drunk whenever she tried to take him around her hippie friends, as if to prove that alcohol was more patriotic than drugs. Most of his attraction for her had been his Italian looks, the cleft in his chin, the premature hairiness, and she also took some pleasure in riling the members of her in-group, who thought they could have some say over the type of person she saw by implying that it was reactionary to date a jock. When she and he found themselves alone, he liked to sit crosslegged on her bed and stroke her cat. They used to read aloud together from his favorite books, *The Prophet* and *Jonathan Livingston Seagull*. She'd never let on to him that anyone else was reading those books, because he thought of them as his personal discovery, something he was turning her on to. The cleft remained, but the hair had thinned almost to baldness, and with the wrinkles under his eyes and the benevolent look on his face, it wasn't difficult to imagine him as somebody's grandfather. Already, he was rehearsing for the role.

He and Mia had a perfect marriage, as far as she could see, and Mia was expecting her second child. They'd had a big Italian wedding, and in their relationship, she managed to be both traditional and liberated. Whenever anyone pointed out the contradictions in her roles, Mia, now in the seventh month of her pregnancy, rolled her big brown eyes, splayed her hands in mock surrender, and putting on an accent, answered, "I'm a woman, what can I say?" Her pregnant breasts were enormous, almost ludicrously so, but she confided to Serena that she was a Victorian at heart. There was something about being pregnant in the summer that made you wish you didn't have breasts at all, so Stefano hadn't really been able to take advantage of her endowments. Stefano unlocked a wooden drawer and reached into an envelope.

"Here, you don't worry about it." He shook his finger. "Just don't tell Mia or she'll be on my case. She'll think I'm keeping a mistress, the way all these macho Italians like her brothers do. She's always telling me I went into the nurturing business as a front. If she asks about the money, I'll tell her I paid a little extra on the house."

"Well, okay, but I am going to pay you back."

"You think I'm worried about it? Something else is bothering you, though."

"I'm fine. I promise, everything is great, we just have unusual house expenses this month."

"Okay, but you know that Mia and me are here for you, huh? You're allowed to feel blue, as long as you can get yourself up enough to come to work. This is a family business. We don't have to pretend to each other we're perfect." He patted her hand in his grandfatherly way. Whatever relations he'd had with her had long since been put into cold storage. He was the only man she knew who never flirted with women. "You want to come have dinner with us? Mia and I don't have any special plans for tonight," he said in a melancholy voice. "God knows what we'll eat, probably something frozen into a block of ice in the freezer last year, but I'm sure we'll have enough of whatever it is."

"Thanks anyway. I have to drive over to Chalk Lake to have supper with my parents, then I'm taking my dad in to get his medications. You'll tell me if any more hours do open up sooner."

"Sure, sure. That's nice the way you take care of your dad. Let's hope our kids take such good care of us when we get older, huh? Give them my regards. I keep meaning to drive over there, but they're so far away now."

On the Mountain Parkway, most of the farmland she passed was high with corn, the flowering tops already visible. In the untilled fields, the tall bluegrass had gone to seed, so that it really did look blue, especially with the sun starting to go down. There weren't usually too many cops along that stretch of road, so she kept the speedometer on eighty, hoping to cut fifteen or twenty minutes off her driving time, so she could lie down on her parents' couch for a few minutes before dinner. No one pulled her over, but her speeding had started to give her a headache as she strained her eyes in the failing light to scan for possible police cruisers parked along the median ahead of her.

Turning off at the exit, she roared through the two little towns lined with beauty shops and car washes, hitting all but one of the green lights, then sped over the mountain past the gravel quarry. There were always dumptrucks pulling in and out of the site, rumbling along at fifteen miles an hour in second gear.

Sure enough, one pulled out in front of her, not even having the decency to let her pass first. The driver must have seen that she was in a hurry, but since his vehicle was bigger than hers, he simply pulled into the road at his leisure, not knowing or caring that someone was barreling around the curve behind him.

She laid on her horn, but if anything, the truck, in response, appeared to trundle even slower. She tried veering into the oncoming lane to go around him, but there were too many curves in the road and no shoulders on the asphalt, and his rig took up two-thirds of the entire road. After several unsuccessful attempts at passing, she came to a long downhill straight stretch and decided to blast around him. Pulling into the oncoming lane, she could see another car approaching in the distance, but there was more than enough time to get around. When she accelerated alongside the dumptruck, it too started to speed up. The wheels on the left side of her car bumped against gravel. "You asshole," she shouted, and floored it. Why in the hell couldn't he let her by? What difference did it make to him whether she was in front of him or behind him? All he wanted to do was mess with her mind to relieve his boredom. The oncoming car was fast approaching, and she had to push the car to its limit, eighty-five miles an hour, its body shaking, before she could eke past the dumptruck far enough to swerve in front of it. The other car blurred by a split second after she had gotten out of its lane. In her rearview mirror, she could see the truck driver flash his headlights at her twice, clicking from the low beam to the high beam and back in a mock gesture of courtesy.

When she had put a few hundred yards as a buffer between them, she eased off the gas and tried to get her breath back. She was trembling, and instead of gradually settling down, the trembling worsened. A spasm rippled in her chest, and the certainty came over her that she was going to die in a couple of seconds from a heart attack. It would kill her before the car even had time to careen off the road and crash. Several seconds went by, and miraculously, she was still alive. Her hands locked on the steering wheel and her arms went completely rigid. She couldn't bend them, not even enough to turn the wheel a single degree.

Summoning every last bit of her shot concentration, she pried her foot from the accelerator and moved it to the brake, fighting gravity the whole time, and through some power she couldn't comprehend, she steered the car over to the grassy edge without flipping it. The dumptruck whooshed by her, its horn blaring. Every last drop of blood seemed to have massed into the left side of her chest, engorging it beyond its capacity to contain. Something was about to explode, her or the car. Flinging the door open, with the motor still running, she leaped into the road without checking for traffic. She sprinted down the incline into a mature cornfield. Slapping the stalks away from her face, one after the next, she ran among the furrows, going deeper and deeper into the field, leaking sweat, trying to put as much distance and as much matter as possible between herself and the car. She lay down in one of the furrows and wrapped her arms tightly around herself, trying to control a shaking and chattering that threatened to knock a tooth out.

There was no telling how many minutes or hours she lay watching an ant struggle with a strand of cornsilk until night came on and she could no longer follow the ant's motion. The chirring of field insects shimmered around her, sending sound waves that buffeted against her skin, making it impossible for her to sit up. A low-level hum swept through the field, as if she were near a power station. The blackness of the night thickened palpably as time went on, filling the spaces between the corn plants, until it had become so viscous it started to seep down into the dirt. Her clothes were covered with a black syrup, rendering her immobile. She couldn't shut her eyelids, and if she did manage to shut them, she felt sure she wouldn't be able to open them again once the eyelashes gummed up. She kept hoping that some wayfarer would come, see her car on the roadside, still running, and figure out that she was lying in the cornfield suffocating. Then they would search for her, find her, and take her to her parents. But no one came, unless someone had already come and gone, taking advantage of the keys in the ignition to steal the car.

With the passage of time, she was able to work herself free of the viscosity and the sound, and she wandered through the corn rows in one direction and another. "A maze of maize," she said, chuckling grimly to herself. "Amazing Grace." She emerged into an open space where she could see her vehicle still parked by the roadside, its headlights illuminated.

Walking ever so slowly, as if any sudden movement on her part might frighten the car the same way the car had frightened her, she gradually stole up on it, walked tentatively around to the driver's side, and slid into the front seat. She clicked on the overhead light. Everything was still in place, as she had left it, even the Diet Cola wedged between the emergency brake and the passenger seat. A cloud of exhaust fumes lingered about the car, and the needle on the temperature gauge had climbed almost up into the red zone, but otherwise, things seemed more or less normal. All the same, she sat in the car for a while, breathing in wisps of carbon monoxide without especially caring what its effect might be, and taking occasional sips of her Coke to dull the acrid taste in her mouth. Two or three cars passed, but they must have assumed she was a parkway traveller reading a road map, because no one stopped to ask her if she had lost her way. She remembered that her father had put several highway flares in the trunk, in case she broke down on the roadside at night. She resolved to put the flares in the floorboard in the back seat. When she had finished her drink and twisted the plastic cap back on, she happened to glance up and notice that the fuel gauge was almost on empty, so she put the car into drive and eased back onto the roadway.

The first frost of the year had covered the garden, the yard, and the overgrown fields with white stubble while she slept. Serena woke early, slipped on jeans and a loose ragg wool sweater, and sauntered onto the back porch holding her coffee cup. She hadn't bothered to brush her hair, which was still sun-bleached but beginning to darken to a honey color. She had stopped highlighting it, and was letting it grow out again. The rhubarb leaves, the flower foliage and the greenery from the tomato plants had curled and stiffened in their beds and had just started to decompose when they were frozen into wizened shapes. Considering how little time she'd been able to devote to the garden, the yield hadn't been bad. None of the summer harvest would be left over to put up for the cold months, but at least she could say she'd provided plenty of vegetables to fill up the table for the season. Ironically, when the produce all started coming in at once, in great abundance, they hadn't been able to eat it fast enough, and couldn't find time to can, so she'd ended up bringing zucchini and tomatoes in to work, and would have taken it to her parents' house as well except that the women in the congregation always brought plenty to church for Josie and Carson during late summer and early fall.

Robbie, still hobbling but able to walk and drive, his wounds healed, and with only a few scars still visible on his cheek and chest, had lost his job at the engineering firm and had taken on temp work until he could find something else. He slept at his parents' place a couple of times a week, rather than make the commute every workday, and Matt, who had gotten employment through his father and was working the zombie shift at the light bulb plant until his royalty checks started coming in, would also crash in town with Robbie from time to time when he was too sleepy to make the long drive back at six in the morning. A lot of the produce had ended up sitting in a basket in the kitchen, rotting before she and Shar could figure out what to do with it.

Measuring out several bucketfuls of feed into the washtub, she hefted it onto one shoulder and picked her way down to the pen. The piglets had already grown to half their mother's size. They snuffled and grunted in anticipation of the feed, the highlight of their day. If she thought about it, it was probably the highlight of hers too. They would be especially excited because she had come down early, but then again they wouldn't have anything else to look forward to until tomorrow. When she rested one end of the washtub atop the wooden fence, the piglets squealed and began to run about, capering with anticipation. Shar had informed her that one of the neighbors down the road had agreed, for a small fee, to slaughter and dress a couple of pigs. Even though they were still undersized, she wanted to go ahead and roast and cure the meat rather than wait until next year. Serena could choose which two if she wanted; if she didn't, Shar would perform the task herself.

Serena couldn't complain. There had been a shortfall of about three hundred dollars on her and Robbie's part each of the first two months, and Shar had made up the difference out of her own dwindling savings. Shar was committed to making it possible for the four of them to stay on the farm. She hadn't made a big deal out of it, but she also wasn't going to put up with any sentimentality about the porcine species. Bending one leg to brace it between the first rail and the washtub, and lifting, Serena dumped the feed in a pile inside the sty. The pigs, clustered around the sow, raced to the pile, bumping each other aside as they rooted. Serena was out of her first trimester. Her penchant for oversized tops and sweaters hadn't called any attention to that fact, because she had always tended to favor loose clothes. Robbie hadn't yet seemed to notice anything out of the ordinary about her figure. Only in the past few days had she started to show. Pretty soon, though, she was going to have to tell everyone. She had a feeling that maybe she had waited too long, and Robbie would leave her, claiming that she had tricked him, which, in truth, she had. That night of their lovemaking was so long ago it was difficult to remember why it had seemed so urgent to conceive.

Dragging the empty washtub over the ground, she walked back up to the porch to have another sip of coffee. It had turned cold. She spat a mouthful onto the rime covering the dirt, and watched it dissolve. On the way to and from work, she had been having as many as three panic attacks per day, where she had to stop the car and run to the roadside. Once a policeman had pulled over to see what was wrong, but by then the terror had passed, and she had gotten to her feet, so she told him it was nothing but a bout of morning sickness, and she hadn't wanted to stain the upholstery.

There was no one she felt comfortable talking to about her predicament, not even her father. Carson would have listened with sympathy, and without passing judgment, but once she had told him, abortion would no longer be an option. He wouldn't forbid it, even if he could, but she knew that within himself he would agonize about it. She was going to have to make up her mind about the abortion very soon, especially if she wanted it performed at the free clinic.

Matt's burnt-orange car came rolling up the drive onto the grass. When he climbed out, still wearing coveralls and holding a thermos loosely in one hand, he had the frowsy look brought on by a combination of too much work and chronic road hypnosis. She knew the feeling well. The firewood ax lay on the grass next to his car, beaded with moisture, and bending to pick it up with his free hand, he tossed it with an easy underhand loop so that it stuck in the stump a few feet away. It was one of his little tricks, one she'd seen him perform many times on camping trips. It had always amused her that he looked so much like a lumberjack and really was good at woodsplitting. Shuffling to the porch, he sank down next to her with a groan. He seemed wearier than usual.

"My warranty is about to expire, I think."

"On your car?"

"Hell, no. On me. Every day I have a new ache." He glanced at the galvanized bucket. "Been out tending your brood?"

"Yeah," said Serena, swirling the coffee in the bottom of the cup. "Preparing them for the slaughter."

Matt slung an arm around her. "You're getting awful maternal these days. Don't worry, we won't make you eat your babies. We're not cannibals. I don't think Shar will really go through with it. It just makes her more secure if she feels like she's got some collateral on the rest of us deadbeats. She keeps threatening to hock my guitar if I don't bring in more cash. Well, somebody's got to be the administrator, and I'm just grateful it ain't me. I'm glad you're up alone so we can spend a few minutes together. I've been missing you. We don't see each other too often these days. I thought about crashing in Robbie's basement, since his folks gave me a spare key, but I decided I'd rather tough out the drive and sleep in my own bed. Well, I guess I should say sleep in your and Robbie's bed, technically speaking."

"Why don't you keep me company for a few more minutes before you rest?"

"Sounds reasonable. Now that I'm here, I don't feel too anxious to go up there, for some reason." Removing a joint from his coverall pocket, he examined it appreciatively. "I think I'll sign off with an early morning smoke. You want to join me?"

"Not at this time of day. It affects me more than it used to."

The weight of Matt's arm on her shoulder made her feel protected. As long as she sat next to him, it would be impossible for her to experience the fear that was becoming an almost daily occurrence. His physical presence warded it off, without his even knowing it. As he gave her a casual, reassuring squeeze, she realized that she had picked the wrong man. It had been within her power to have either one of them, him or Robbie, and if she had only overcome her scruples and allowed Matt to keep kissing her that night in the bedroom above the leather shop, she never would have let herself become involved with Robbie, and she wouldn't be pregnant by him now.

"Did old Robbie sleep in Lexington last night?"

"Yes. He's doing it more often these days. I cry out in my sleep, and he can't get any rest."

Matt exhaled a mouthful of sweet smoke. "He's not used to so much responsibility. None of us are, really. But he's usually starting to think of the slopes in Utah about this time of year. His seasonal migration. It's going to take him a while to adjust to a new way of life. Me and Shar been together for years and years, and we're still trying to figure it out ourselves."

"At first he was really sympathetic and sweet about my insomnia. He'd sit up in bed and rub my neck until I fell asleep. Sometimes it happens to me two or three times in a night. I have such intense dreams. But after the first few times, it started getting on his nerves. He told me he'd never been an insomniac, he'd always gone right off as soon as he hit the pillow, and that I was making him one. I never should have believed him when he said he wanted to settle down. I think he blames me for the fact that he's stuck. Do I seem weird to you?"

Matt laughed. "Compared to what?"

"I don't know. Do I act bizarre? I feel like I'm not a very good judge of my own behavior any more."

"No." He had on his face the contemplative and slightly bemused look of a stoned person. "Well, once in a while, when we're kidding around, it seems a little forced on your part."

"I'm forced? My laughter is artificial?"

"Don't get anxious about it. All of us are worn to the nub, not only you." Flicking ashes onto the ground, he rubbed them into the dirt with his workboot, crunching a latticework of frost beneath his feet.

"But I seem artificial to you?"

"No, no. I never used that word."

"Forced, then. Wasn't that what you said?"

"I'm sorry I said anything. Look, you wouldn't seem forced to me, because I know you. We don't have any pretenses. I only meant that if somebody else was here, say a stranger, somebody we didn't know, and we were having a party out here at the farm, they might perceive you as being, I don't know, strained, like maybe you're not enjoying yourself as much as you want them to believe."

"But you must have noticed something strained about me yourself, or you wouldn't be able to say that."

Matt gave a heavy sigh. "You know what? I'm dead on my feet. I don't really have the energy or the wits for this conversation."

"Of course, sure. I'm sorry to corner you, Matt. I am nervous."

"If you're up for the day, would you mind if I crashed on your bed? It would be nice to sleep in my own real bed again, if only for one day. I don't want to wake Shar if she's still asleep."

"You look kind of sad yourself. Tired, is that all?"

He shook his head, looking down between his knees at the ground. "Me and Shar are going to be needing to split up again."

"You're leaving the farm? And her?"

"I don't know. I'll still turn over as much of my paycheck to her as I can, to keep up my part, or maybe I'll make a bed in the living room. I haven't decided. She thinks I'm only staying with her out of pity, and I'm tired of trying to convince her that I love her. We've talked so much about the semantics of it, I don't even know what I feel any more. What the fuck is love anyway? Even though she's stayed in remission for over a year, all she can see herself as is a walking nest of cancer, and she's biding her time, waiting for it to reappear. She can run rapids on the river, heft a basket of clothes over her head and carry it upstairs, hoe, cook, drive tenpenny nails. She's a pioneer woman, but she thinks of herself as an invalid. I can't hack that too much longer. She's to the point, in her mind, that it doesn't make any difference what I say. Plus, when she hears my other news, she's going to blow her stack completely."

"What news?"

"Ah, you'll find out soon enough. I've known for a few days, but I couldn't quite make up my mind to tell her, or any of you guys. I feel terrible about the whole thing."

"What is it? You can confide in me."

"No, because you're going to be upset with me too."

"I won't. Whatever it is, I forgive you in advance. There's nothing you can do to make me angry. You don't know how much good it does me just to sit on this porch with you. Anyway, I have a secret of my own. We'll trade secrets. Why don't you bring your guitar out? I'd love to hear you play one of your new compositions. Or I'll come in the room with you." She stroked his hair, and let her hand wander to his neck. "We can sit on the bed, like in the old days, and shut the door, and I'll listen while you strum, and we'll talk about what design I'm going to make for your first album cover. I still plan to make good on that offer. I'm going to make good on everything I said I'd do."

He hesitated, considering, giving her a searching look. At last, he took her hand, squeezed it, and gently let it drop. "Maybe another day." He stood up.

"I'll tell you my secret anyway. I'm going to have a baby."

For a few beats, Matt gave her a stupid, deliberate, uncomprehending look. "That's beautiful," he said, his voice barely audible. "I'm happy for you guys. I always wanted to be Uncle Matt. Pick the gee-tar by the crib." He opened the screen door. "Does Shar know yet?"

"No. Robbie doesn't either. You're the only person in the world I've told. Hypothetically, anybody could be the father. Anybody who wanted to claim responsibility. I was planning on breaking the news this week. I just hadn't decided exactly what I was going to say."

His breathing quickened, puffs of it in the cold air. The toe of his boot toyed with a loose piece of weatherstripping in the doorframe. "Right. Right. I'll study on it. I got to get out here and replace this insulation, or else the wind's going to whistle through the cracks all winter long."

She heard him walk across the kitchen floor and into the living room with his heavy tread. Then he retraced his steps, and through the screen door, she could see him sit down on her bed and slide each boot off with the opposite foot. He set his acoustic guitar on his lap. For a few minutes, he strummed, not really playing a tune, only pieces of this and that, trailing off into something else after a few bars.

Then came his voice, soft but clear. It carried further than she would ever have imagined such a voice could. "On a summer's day in the month of May, a big burly boy come a-hiking. Down a shady lane near the sugar cane, he was looking for his liking. As he strolled along, he sang a song, of the land of milk and honey, where a boy can stay for many a day, and he won't need any money. Oh, the buzzing of the bees and the cigarette trees, the soda water fountain, where the bluebird sings to the lemonade springs, in the big rock candy mountain."

She closed her eyes and mouthed the words as she listened to him sing. "In the big rock candy mountain, the cops have wooden legs, the bulldogs all have rubber teeth, the hens lay soft boiled eggs, the farmer's trees are full of fruit, the barns are full of hay. I want to go where there ain't no snow, where the sleet don't fall, and the wind don't blow, in that big rock candy mountain."

He was a troubador. He should have existed centuries ago, before the days of recording contracts and sound studios. An image of Bett as a young girl lying in bed came to her, clearer and more vivid than any memory she'd ever experienced. Bett's hair had natural black ringlets in it, ones Serena was running her hands through, and skin so tender that Serena's own delicate, pubescent skin felt rough by comparison when they rubbed their cheeks together. After she had sung, she lay down next to the little girl until she fell asleep, and even then she lingered, listening to the rhythm of Bett's insect breath, as she inhaled and exhaled through sensual, perfect, unknowing lips. If Matt would only keep on singing, he would never have to tell his news, and she wouldn't have to reveal her secret to anyone else. But she knew how many verses were in the song, and in a few seconds, it would be over.

The stairs creaked, and she heard Shar's voice, low, inquiring. He kept strumming scraps of song as he answered, the way he often did to avoid looking at the person he was talking to. Little by little, the pitch of the conversation rose. Then he spoke, and there was a long silence. Shar started crying, and between sobs, accused him of something. He didn't answer, didn't try to defend himself. She repeated the same intonation, and after a pause, he gave her a terse answer. Shar went into the kitchen, ran water in the sink, and rattled the leftover dishes from last night. Then a glass broke, and another one. The screen door opened, banged. Without looking up, she caught a glimpse of Shar's pointy-toed, second-hand shoes, a size too big for her.

"I suppose you know that Matt's contract with the music company has been canceled."

"No, I didn't. How can they cancel a contract?"

"Apparently, it was only a verbal agreement. I don't know

how he did it, but Matt had me snowed into believing he was really going to cash in for at least tens of thousands. He kept telling me that he was going to take care of me, and that sounded so sweet, the idea of being taken care of, that I let myself go against my instincts and agreed to buy this place. I wanted to let go, and fall in a soft spot for once in my life. They talked to him about a contract over the phone, and kept promising they would send it as soon as they had the details worked out, but they never sent one. They shopped a couple of his songs around. Nobody ended up taking them, so last week they mailed him a check for fifty dollars and returned the song sheets and his cassette. That means that for the foreseeable future, the four of us are each making barely above minimum wage, and you're not even working full time. We'll have to file for bankruptcy."

"Bankruptcy? Couldn't we sell the farm?"

Shar rolled her eyes. "Am I the only one around here who understands anything about how the world works? The problem with the three of you is that you're hippies. I hate to tell you this, but hippies are extinct. They outlived their limited usefulness. Natural selection did them in. Why do you think that guy gave us this farm at such a good price, and was eager to finance it himself? You don't know? That never occurred to you? Because we're in a deep recession. Which means nobody is going to snap this place up. Like us, it's an anachronism. Even if we could hold on for months while we put it on the market, which we can't afford to do, we'd have to let it go at a substantial loss to ourselves. You're looking downhearted, Serena. None of this should be news to you. Matt said he's known for a few days about the music contract, but naturally, this is the first I'm hearing about it. I don't doubt that you're his usual confidante."

"This is the first I've heard, I swear it. He did say he was going to talk to you about something, but he didn't let on what it was."

"Don't lie to me, Serena. Just because I'm going to die doesn't mean I'm out to lunch. Or that I can be taken advantage of by everyone. I've spent most of my funeral money on this stupid farm, so when I go, there won't be enough left to bury me, and I suppose Matt will just dig a grave somewhere beyond the garden plot to economize. But then you three will be out one bookkeeper, right when you need me most."

Serena stood up to embrace her. "You're not going to die. You're in remission."

"Don't come near me. You don't know the first thing about it. You've been fucking Matt, haven't you?"

"What?"

"You heard me. With Robbie in Lexington so much, and me at the leather shop until late, all of us coming and going at odd hours, it's not that difficult. And then he lounges in plain sight on your bed downstairs after the two of you have fucked. You could at least have the courtesy not to rub my face in it."

"He asked if he could sleep there because he saw me out here working. It's your all's bed."

"Don't think I'm not on to your little piece of business, either. You're pregnant. I know a pregnant woman when I see one, and you're definitely one. Does Robbie know?"

Serena was too taken by surprise to deny the accusation. "I don't see what that has to do with anything."

"I'll answer the question for you. I asked him a couple of days ago, and he said that if you were, it was news to him. If he hasn't asked you about it since then, it's probably because he's afraid to find out the answer. He probably suspects that the baby isn't his. Is Matt the father? I want to hear you deny it straight out. I want to hear you lie to my face."

Serena studied Shar a long moment before answering. Whichever answer she gave, she couldn't retract it afterward. "What did Matt say when you asked him?"

"He denied it of course, and told me the two of you had never gone to bed together. He wants to spare me the humiliation. I suppose I can't blame him too much, since he wasn't getting any satisfaction from me. It was bound to happen sooner or later. I just wish it had been with somebody else, somebody in town who

I'd never met before, one of his little groupies from the Jefferson Davis Inn."

"Matt is completely faithful to you. I can tell you he's the most loyal person I know. He's had his opportunities with women, but he's never gone through with them. I know you and I have never gotten along very well, but I want to give you one piece of advice, and I'm trying to speak as a friend. We're losing everything. Everything is slipping through our fingers. Don't throw Matt away, now that you need him most. Don't do that to yourself. He's the only person in this world you can trust."

Shar stumbled blindly down the yard, looking desperately about, as if she had left something important outside, something that would solve everything if she could only remember what it was and find it. Her eye fell on the axe in the stump, and reaching out, she wrenched it free and ran toward the barn, her ample skirts swirling behind. "Don't hurt yourself," Serena cried out. "Oh, God. Oh, Christ." Serena started to bolt after her, but decided to call for Matt first. When she turned to open the screen door, he was already on his way outside. "I think she's going to do something to herself," she said. The two of them sprinted after her, the frosted grass crackling beneath their feet. She was surprisingly fast, a lot faster than Serena would have guessed from the almost arthritic way she had of moving about the house. Shar climbed the wooden fence, lifting her skirt and leaping over the rail to land square in the frozen muck, on her feet.

The pigs were in a frenzy. At first they must have thought they were about to get an unexpected second feeding, so soon after their first, but then they scurried about in different directions, slipping on icy patches, not knowing where to run. For a few seconds, Shar chased them, busting the surface of the icy puddles with her heels, running in a circle like an agitated colt. Then she stood dead still in the middle of the sty, turning her head slowly, the axe limp by her side, unthreatening, as if stalking a canny fly. The sow had backed into a corner and lay down with a fatalistic sigh. The pigs slowed their movement, watching her through the slits in their eyes and puffing up their sides. Their expressions were intelligent. Shar, too, breathed hard, pressing a palm against her waist. Serena lifted one leg over the fence. In two quick strides, Shar was upon one of the pigs, riding it to the ground with the weight of her body. The axe cleaved deep into its side, and blood flowed across the solid ripples of hard, packed dirt. Squealing, the pig wallowed, trying in desperation to dislodge the axe. The other piglets kept their distance, turning their bodies sideways to their wounded sibling as its life ebbed out. The sow watched its dying spasms with an air of indifference. Clambering out of the pen, the pleats in her skirt smeared with blood, Shar stood next to Serena, with her eyes still fastened on the last of the spectacle. Then she looked Serena in the face, the dark circles under her eyes absorbing another layer of shade. "You pick the other one," she said, and started back toward the farmhouse with her slow, labored, accustomed gait.

Matt and Robbie were trying to take Lila's oak bedstead down the stairs, the one Serena had brought over from Chalk Lake on the assumption that it would never have to be moved again. It was extraordinarily heavy, and made so that it didn't come apart. They had the bed turned on its side, and had to keep resting every couple of steps to keep it from sliding and crushing Matt. A bandage wrapped around his knee, Robbie was determined to continue lifting heavy furniture, the way he had all his life, no matter what the consequences. His youth wasn't going to be wrested from him except by main force. He was singing, out of tune but with forced gaiety, I come from Alabama with a bandage on my knee.

After Matt's two weeks on the couch, he and Shar had made up, in their own peculiar way. He'd returned upstairs, and now they were going to move back to Chevy Chase together. Having declared bankruptcy and failed in every area of their aspirations seemed to restore them to equanimity, as though they were relieved not to have anything more to strive for. He had put his guitar away in its case, and hadn't touched it since. Shar treated him with more affection than before, making sure his coveralls were clean for work, and tiptoeing around the house while he slept during the day.

Serena couldn't help thinking that if she and Robbie had continued to sleep in that bed, things might have taken a different turn for themselves. Robbie injected the baby into almost every conversation, trying to be casual about it, to lull her and everybody else, including her parents, into a false sense of security. He'd gone with her to her parents' to tell them she was expecting. They hadn't reacted quite the way she'd anticipated. They were very cordial to Robbie, as if they were afraid the least hesitation on their part would frighten him off. After dinner, Carson had gone on a walk with Robbie around the lake, laboring along on his cane, something he hardly ever did anymore, and she had the feeling that the two of them, along with Josie, were conspiring against her, that she was somehow being humored. They subtly treated Robbie as if he were the one with sound judgment, and she his ward, and they only wanted to make sure above all that he would keep an eye on her. Neither of them had seemed upset, as they should have been, about the money she'd squandered on the down payment. No doubt they'd decided to swallow it, to write it off as one more loss on her account, or maybe Robbie and her father had worked out some plan for gradual repayment once Robbie was able to find engineering work, get them settled, and make good on their remaining debts to restore their credit. He was suddenly obsessed by the thought that he might have acquired a bad credit record. The conversation at dinner had centered not on the baby, not on her and Robbie's plans for their new life, but on her.

Her mother asked if she had started seeing a therapist yet, when she already knew the answer, and tried to hand her a couple of names she'd found out, but Serena had knocked the piece of paper to the floor, and Robbie had ended up picking it up and putting it into his pocket. The day she'd confessed to Robbie that she'd conceived on purpose, without telling him, they had a huge fight, in which he'd gotten so upset he smashed the alarm clock by hurling it against the wall, and called her a conniving bitch. He'd tried to live a normal life with her, he'd really given it his best shot, but he'd had it with her night sweats and anxieties.

If it was a question of child support, and if she refused to get an abortion, naturally he'd pay, but he wasn't going to sacrifice the rest of his life just because he'd happened to make the stupid mistake of driving her home from a bar one night. She answered that it didn't make any difference which one she did, because she was probably going to kill herself anyway. He'd shouted that she wasn't going to get her way by making spectacular threats. She kept hoping he would hit her, but he didn't. Instead, he stormed out of the house, and went off somewhere, maybe some redneck country tavern, and rolled in at two in the morning, his beery breath reeking as he collapsed into the bed.

The next morning, hungover, he'd seemed fragile and contrite. After drinking raw eggs and going for a swim in the cold river, he sat down with her at the kitchen table and asked her to forgive him for everything he'd said the night before. He didn't think right now was a very good time for her to go through the ordeal of an abortion, now that he'd had a chance to reflect on it. He was just unused to the idea of being a father, it was new to him, but there was nothing to do about their situation now except see it through, and he assured her he would grow used to the idea in time. He kept patting her hand and asking her if she felt better this morning too. More than anything, he seemed really scared of what she might do. He didn't bring up the threat she'd made, he was careful not to, it was almost absurd how neither of them even said the word, but that was when he'd suggested they should go over and talk to her parents, to try to get everything straightened out.

But she was onto the scam. Just as they started to pack their possessions, Robbie told her that once they vacated the farm, he was going to take a little winter camping trip for a week or so, to try to get his head together, and that she could stay with her parents, who had agreed to put her up until he returned and found them an apartment in Lexington. She didn't know whether her parents were in on the scheme, or whether he was duping them too, but she had a feeling that once he got out to the Rockies, he wasn't coming back, and they probably had a psychiatrist lined up for her to see. Well, he could make whatever plans he wanted, but she had plans of her own.

She wandered into the kitchen to finish packing a few of the items left in the cabinet, spices and Tupperware. It was pathetic how few possessions they collectively owned, the four of them, once they were packed into a fourteen-foot truck. When she filled a box, and started to carry it outside, Robbie came in, as he'd been doing all morning, and told her not to lift anything, as if she were some Southern belle from the nineteenth century in confinement, and he her doting chevalier, the one who carried women up flights of stairs instead of carrying their bedsteads down flights of stairs. "I'm fine," she said. "It isn't heavy, and I'm not that far along yet."

"I'll be the judge of that. Are you about ready for me to take you over to your folks? Me and Matt have got to get this stuff into storage before the place closes for the afternoon. I told him I'd meet him there."

"I'm not going to Chalk Lake tonight. I want to sleep here one more time before I give up this farm for good."

"I don't think so. I promised your Dad and Mom I'd drop you off over there today."

"So I'll call them and tell them I plan to come tomorrow instead. My car is here, after all, and if you take me, then my father will have to drive all the way over here with his bad leg so we can retrieve it. That's not too thoughtful of you."

"Well, there's no phone here. It was disconnected this morning."

"There's a pay phone at the grocery, in the parking lot. I am an adult, in case you've forgotten." He remained looking at her, trying to conceal his worried expression. "What do you think I'm going to do? Well? Speak up."

"Nothing. I don't think you're going to do anything."

"If that were in my mind, don't you imagine I could engineer a way to do it easily enough? Do you really suppose your dropping me off at my parents' would prevent me? All you're interested in is absolving yourself of responsibility, in case something does happen. But if you were really that worried, you wouldn't be trekking off to Colorado in the first place, right?"

"I told you, I'm coming back. I'm not going to go into all this again right now. The aftermath of filing for bankruptcy has completely wracked my nerves, and I have to have some time alone."

"To do what? Meditate on your credit record?"

"You know that's not it. This is the last chance I'll have for a long time to winter camp and spend time just with myself. I know you don't believe me. But it's true. It's fine if you want to stay here one more night," he said, trying to sound nonchalant. "Like sleeping in a monastery. The heat will be on, and the lights, because they're not cutting the electricity until tomorrow. I'll leave the mattress we were going to throw out, and a couple of blankets and a pillow. This can be your camping trip, your time alone. Afterward, we'll compare notes. When me and Matt are done dropping this stuff, I'll call your parents from Lexington. Let me do at least that, not because I don't trust you, but because I told them you'd be there, and I don't want them to think I blew it off. Okay? I'm already on your dad's shit list for knocking you up." He leaned over to kiss her, and she let him, but she couldn't bring herself to return the kiss with any passion. "Serena, I know you're royally pissed about me going to the Rockies, but we've got the rest of our lives to figure out this situation. One week isn't going to make or break us."

"You're right," she said. "We've got the rest of our lives." She tucked his hair, which had grown out, behind his ears, like a wife inspecting her husband before he goes off to work, and carried the box out among the snow flurries to the moving van.

Early that evening, as soon as the hypothetical sunset took place, because there hadn't been any sun visible to set, only a gray haze that thickened into a gradual eclipse, a snowstorm hit hard, the first of the season, premature. Gusts beat the panes while she walked about, staring out now one curtainless window, now another, wiping fog from the glass, watching the pastureland fill up with snow. Sleet pinged off the windows. Though the house was empty except for the mattress and a couple of plastic bags of forgotten garbage, she turned the lights on in all of the rooms, upstairs and down. From the outside, at a distance, it must look as though a glorious celebration were in progress, as though a group of people were nestled inside in warmth and fellowship, eating good food, drinking wine, and commenting on how grateful they were to be sheltered from the inclement weather.

Robbie would be in Denver by now, situated in his bedroll in the youth hostel, rubbing his wounded knee, denying the pain he was in, talking about ultimate Frisbee with some guy in the bunk below. It was ironic that he'd gone all the way to Colorado to winter camp, when if he'd stayed, he would have had a wilderness of snow at his fingertips. Nothing could be easier than to lose oneself in the deeps of their two hundred acres, the wild land they had never explored properly, never taken advantage of the way they'd promised themselves. She hadn't even returned to the waterfall she'd found by chance on their first trek around the farm. It couldn't be terribly far off, but somehow or another, none of them had run across it again.

Struggling into her down parka, cap, gloves, boots, she walked onto the back porch and pulled the door shut behind her until the safety lock clicked. She had to tread with exaggerated care to keep from slipping on the wafer-thin ice on the back porch. It was the type of ice that elderly women who live alone slip on and break their hips when they're taking out the garbage in the middle of the night, because they have insomnia and are looking for something to occupy their mind. She trudged through the fresh snow, dragging her feet the way a child does, making tracks, the only set of tracks on her vast tract of acreage.

The flake-filled air and the lack of light made it impossible to tell with any precision which direction she was heading.

There was no way she'd ever find the waterfall, except through divine intervention. She should wander among the leafless branches, looking for a sign, counting on deliverance. Wasn't that the way they did things in the Old Testament, in grand style, so that if deliverance was withheld, they didn't just die, they perished? The cable at the river came into her mind. All it would take was one running swing, and then the release, as she completed the gesture she had begun back in the summer. The river wasn't frozen, only icy enough to preserve her for as long as necessary until a crew could fish her out. That was the one direction she could go, downhill, without resistance, without losing her way. If Matt's hoe handle had really swelled, the way he'd bragged, there would be a highway to make things even easier and clearer, but even without it, when you were lost, the one sure way to find where you were was to seek water. Even the wind blew in that direction.

She knew she was playing a deadly game, but it was one she couldn't resist playing. One part of her goaded the other on, making dares, seeing how far it could go and still come back, and she had always been one to take dares. Her entire life had been a dare of one kind or another, and this was its logical final expression. How many times could you contemplate your death before you used up all your chances? Fifty? A hundred? Did the odds increase each time you thought about it, or was it like what they said about a miscarriage, that having one in no way affected the probability of conceiving the next time around?

If she had been seeing a counselor, as her mother had suggested, he or she—probably he—would be asking her if she was having specific thoughts, that was the crucial phrase, and when he asked if she was having specific thoughts, she could entertain him with some grisly gothic description, some good old Appalachian folklore all about mountain women being strangled and beaten and hacked and maimed and suffocated down by the willow garden, the way they deserved for being such chaste, pious, innocent, blushing, virginal, alabaster, cocksucking sluts. She was sure she could keep the therapist's juices flowing enough so that he would keep her alive from visit to visit, a Scheherazade sick in the head, and no matter how empathetic, dynamic, transactional, gestalt, he purported to be and meant to be, no matter how devoted to her complete and total self-actualization, when she got through with him he would go home and jack off on his bedstead with images of her battered body dancing in his head and a box of scented tissues close at hand, because all men, even the nice ones, especially the nice ones, got off on that kind of talk.

She knew that if she kept up in this vein, opening this vein, much longer, she was certain to push herself over the edge, in the most literal way. The cable pulsated in her mind, each of its fibers meshed in a design so precise it seemed foreordained. Nothing could stop it from dangling from the tree like a hangman's rope in its inviting, beckoning verticality, the last few feet of it snaking along the bank for easy access, kept in place by its own weight, so that even the bitter winds wouldn't blow it out of her reach. She knew that it would be there. Robbie hadn't put up a struggle about leaving her alone overnight, and her parents had obviously decided to trust her judgment and not drive out to the farm on icy roads on the off chance that she might be as deranged as she acted, because despite all their fretting, they had always had far too much confidence in her powers of reason.

She was really starting to scare the hell out of herself. The faster her thoughts ran, the faster she walked. She was hurrying down the hillside, unable to slow her precipitous, overexcited motion, like Jill who came tumbling after, and she had to throw her body into the snow, like someone who has caught fire by accident, stop, drop, and roll, as they had taught her in elementary school, straight into a bramble bush to stop her progress. Flakes drifted above her, touching her face. Despite the storm clouds, the air sparkled with mineral brightness. Silence abounded. Even her breath remained so muffled it sank back into her of its own weight. With the infinitesimal wisp of sanity still adrift within her, she had to climb the hill, force herself into the car, and drive the sixty miles to Chalk Lake, so she could give up the ghost to someone who might know what to do with it. She had to drive with the foreknowledge that no one but her would be out on the road on a night like this, and that if she were so overcome on the way that she had to pull over and vanish into a snowy field like a white rabbit on a white background, down into its white burrow, there wouldn't be anyone to stop her, because she was a grown woman and free to do as she pleased.

The climb up her parents' driveway was so steep it had to be made in first gear with the pedal to the floor, and if you slowed for even an instant, especially in winter, you were lost. Her car shuddered its way to the top, and the engine died just as she rounded the bend onto the level stretch. She pulled the emergency brake and got out. The cabin was dark. Inside, no mutthound stirred under the bed, and her parents had left no note. She wouldn't leave one either. It would only give them a false clue to try to decipher in the years to come, however many years they had left, as they racked their brains to figure out what they could have said or done differently to change the outcome. She thought about calling Kelsey, to have a quick conversation, but then Kelsey might discern from her tone of voice that something was badly wrong, and would try to calm her down. A bottle of cranberry juice had been left out on the counter. She took a swig from it, and put it back in the refrigerator so it wouldn't turn warm. Pulling the door to, and making sure it was locked, she took the outside stairs down, rather than the driveway, so she wouldn't slip and hurt herself. Across the road lay the pier.

The pitch of the wood sounded unusually low beneath her heels as she walked the length of the pier to its edge. She'd never consciously thought of wood as having a pitch before, but of course it did. Everything did, everything was acoustic, it was simply a matter of noticing it. It must either have to do with the temperature of the wood or the amount of moisture in it. The

Canadian geese had abandoned the lake for the winter, headed for parts unknown. Did the same geese come back every year, or was it their offspring, and if so, by what instinct did they know to return to Chalk Lake? She had no idea what was the life span of a goose.

A cap of snow had covered the overturned rowboat like cream-cheese frosting. Off to her right lay the cottage of the man who did repairs, kept the land around the lake mowed, cleared deadwood that fell on the service road during storms, and looked after the cabins in the off-season, when the summer people went back to town. Her parents were one of few families who lived on the lake year around. She tried to remember the watchman's name. It was on the tip of her tongue, but she would never think of it now. Sitting on the edge of the dock, legs dangling, the way she did when she fished, she removed her gloves, tossed them in the water, and watched them disappear as the wool became saturated. Her father still hadn't replaced the broken ladder. There were certain idiosyncracies he clung to, sins of omission, and no matter what anybody thought or said, or how often they nagged him about it, he simply wasn't going to change his mind. For somebody who believed in the hand of Providence, he sure could be a willful son of a gun. Ladder or no ladder, she wasn't going to enter the lake any more the way the dogs did. She stood up and removed her down parka, in case its air pockets might prove too buoyant.

III

≈

Shall Your lovingkindness be declared in the grave? Or Your faithfulness in the place of destruction? Shall Your wonders be known in the dark? And Your righteousness in the land of forgetfulness?

—Psalm

〰 She wasn't sure by what instinct she'd gotten to her father's church. She was soaking wet, clothes crepitating, hands chapped and rigid, the tang of brackish water in her nostrils and mouth and burning throat. But she knew this was her father's church, from the sunken plot of land on which it sat, the horizontal stripes of its white boards tapering to a vanishing point, the sharp slant in the roof's black pitch, the barren weeping willows along one side in a windrow separating the building from the frozen tobacco field beyond, the gravestones that littered the dooryard like so many broken teeth. Ice sheathed the road, and even with her hiking boots on, she had a hard time scrabbling across. Possibly she'd left her car listing in a drainage ditch and hitchhiked. Looking behind and beside, she couldn't make out where she might have abandoned it. Only road and field loomed, running together gray to black, without a shoulder.

Rock salt had been scattered along the church driveway, plentiful as a shower of rice, and as she stumbled down the incline, chunks of the salt lodged in the crevices of her soles. A surprising number of vehicles filled the parking spaces closest to the church, considering the weather, too many for a Wednesday service, not quite enough for a Sunday, so she couldn't say for sure which day it might be. In the glassed-in marquee, the legend said Being a Regular Baptist, and the name beneath it was Rev. Robert C. "Bob" Mayo, the superfluous nickname in quotation marks so cheerful, so heedless of her gaze upon its unearned familiarity that she almost didn't go in, except she had to seek shelter because she had lost the feeling in her toes and hands and shook without ceasing. She might have been outdoors for hours and hours, for all she knew, close to frostbite.

It was odd to pay attention to details like that when in no time she would cease to exist, without sensation, a numb more permanent than frostbite, deeper into the bone, so complete it wouldn't be felt, not even as the absence of feeling. She couldn't keep herself in the water, so she was going to let the water come to her. But she couldn't lie down in a gully and wait for a drift to smother her until she had at least caught sight of her father first, for one last look, he, her alpha and omega even though she would forever not hold fast to the memory of that look. I'll never see you again never never never not ever, she couldn't say it enough not enough for now to last for all eternity even though her every indivisible instant was already eternity. She tried to multiply eternity times eternity to see if her mind could hold it so she'd have a foretaste of how it would feel not to be because what she wanted more than anything right now was a dress rehearsal of her irrevocable extinction to see whether or not it felt better than she did in case she might change her mind later even though she didn't want to change it and knew she wouldn't change it except she wanted to know how to stop all of everything without stopping it herself.

From the mud room where the coats were hung and overshoes discarded, trying to work the knot out of her left hiking boot with clumsy fingers, she could hear the four-part harmonies a cappella of her father and his three deacons. Her musical ear remained intact, perfect, a single delicate mechanism inside her, the only one not warped. One of the deacons sang strident and off-key like always and the other three voices, including her father's tenor, remained unvarnished, with no vibrato, plaintive, hard, nasal, each phrase unexpectedly smoothing out at its end like a sigh of relief.

> *We're near to Canaan's happy shores*
> *That place so bright and fair*
> *Thank God we'll never sin again*
> *There'll be no sorrow there.*

The bass of one of the deacons repeated there would be no sorrow be no sorrow there, hitting low notes that rumbled away beyond her range of hearing. By the time she'd pulled off her shoes and slid into the backmost pew in her sock feet, soaked with lake water and melted snow, the quartet had vanished, and a man she didn't recognize, tall, strapping in the gangly way of mountain men, white-haired, with copious liver spots, horn-rimmed glasses, sinews in his forearms, had gripped both sides of the podium as if he meant to hoist it above his head as a proof of strength.

Her father, seated behind and to one side, had on bifocals as he scanned a worn volume she recognized as a Greek Old Testament with a nameplate from 1910 inscribed with someone's name neither of them had ever heard of. *This book belongs to Mrs. Wesley Strode.* She'd urged him to buy it the last time they visited the used bookstore together, joking with him that no one else would ever buy it if he didn't and it would sit on the shelf for another fifty years, while Mrs. Wesley Strode receded further into oblivion. The cane was nowhere in sight, but she could make out the withered foreleg beneath the pants. His head downcast, he nodded to himself as was his habit in the days when he'd squeeze in behind the kitchen table to read, listening to music on a transistor radio almost always with the speaker laid face down so that it distorted the classical music he loved in his undiscriminating and ardent way. Looking up, he gave the room at large an absent thoughtful stare, gauging the middle distance so no one in the congregation would be left out of his all-inclusive inwardness.

A voice not his began to preach. "My text for tonight, which comes to me only as I speak, is drawed from the Book of Job, chapter fourteen, verses ten through twelve. But man dies, and is laid low; man breathes his last, and where is he? As waters fail from a lake, and a river wastes away and dries up, so man lies down and rises not again; until the heavens are no more, he will not awake, or be roused out of his sleep. I thank Brother Carson for having me to Bethel as guest pastor for this late service. I've never darkened the door of a seminary, so I'm not what some would call a right man of the cloth in the same sense as him, but many's the time I've wanted to address Brother Carson's flock. I have no education, and I am verily almost illiterate in spite of my advanced age. But my congregation is large, and grows apace each week. Every man that God wants to preach, He calls him if it is fitten. If ye didn't know the first letter of creation, if ye was ignorant of Genesis and Revelation, if ye knew not the lamentations of Job and yet God blesses ye to preach, you'll preach plime blank what he wishes ye to. You'll preach the gospel right out. A preacher mounts the pulpit and he don't make up what he shall preach aforehand. Ye have to get shut of this natural mind of yourn afore ye can proclaim the Gospel of Jesus Christ.

"I started out to do right and the Devil hindered me. That's the gospel truth. I was a bad man, but always desirous that the Lord would forgive me. I couldn't give up the world, for I loved the world too much. But you can't love nothing of the world. Hit holds nothing for ye. Otherways you shall perish, and no remedy. The Lord saw fit to afflict me with cancer. He brought me low. Five tumors growed in my body the size of hailstones, them kind that trammeled the corn fields about twelve year ago, afore Brother Carson come to these parts. I knew I was guilty, worthy of my ill luck, but still yet I couldn't pray, I only cursed and moaned. The name of the Lord was defiled in my very mouth. I reckoned shore I was bound for torment and couldn't shun it noways. A man has to suffer all before he can enter into the Kingdom of God.

"I have drunk some liquor in my time. I've played the fiddle and cursed. It is in the sixth chapter of Numbers, I recollect, that we are commanded to shun strong drink. That's Old Bible. Yet since the Lord opened my eyes, and answered my prayers, I have had nary bit of desire to drink strong spirits. The Lord is my doctor now. If people would live right and have faith, they wouldn't have to run to the doctor so much and they wouldn't shorten their days. You can do right and God will lengthen them. He will do it. I asked him to take my affliction away, and after six weeks, the tumors was removed. The Lord may strike me down tomorrow, or see fit to return each tumor to its rightful place at any moment. No one knows the hour nor the day. If I don't suffer for Christ, I hain't been raised with him. That is all there is to it. I have did what I could through the power of prayer. I have uttered what I did not understand, things too wonderful for me, which I did not know, Job forty two. His will be done."

Her father had kept his head bowed. He, so mild and ecumenical, so reluctant to criticize, detested charismatic preaching and faith healing. Why had he let this man come into his church and insult him to his face? The insinuation was that if Carson only had more faith, he could be rid of his cancer too. If he stayed sick, it was a weakness in him. But that wasn't true. No one had more faith than Carson, yet he'd been stricken down, while this self-serving son of a bitch got lucky. He'd gotten fucking lucky, that's all, and he didn't have sense enough to understand that, he had to go around from church to church proclaiming his superior righteousness after the fact. She wished the man's tumors would come back tenfold, the size of golf balls, to take him down a peg or two.

She wanted to curse God and die. She didn't believe in God and yet she was angry at Him, the God of her father, the God of Abraham and Isaac and Jacob and the whole shitload of gullible descendants who inhabited those endless goddamned genealogies in the Old Testament, the ones she'd always skipped over. Each and every one of them was a name on a gravestone, the roll call down here, not up there. They had perished believing in an afterlife right up to the last second, and that comforting lie was their reward, their paradise, as it would also be her father's.

Carson's biggest frustration was that he hadn't been able to give faith to her on a chromosome, the way he'd given her his oversized sloping Irish nose. Kelsey didn't attend church, but when asked, she said yes she believed in God, she just didn't think that much about it. For her, it was like answering the census bureau's query whether you were male or female. Kelsey had lucked out, she'd been the one to get the faith chromosome. It was difficult for Serena to disappoint her father, as she tried in vain year after year to explain to him that even if you wanted to believe with all your heart and all your soul, you couldn't just make yourself when the seed of terminal skepticism had been planted in your mind through a process you didn't even understand. She might as well wish not to have panic attacks as to have faith, for all the good it did her.

Carson was forever trying to offer her an analogy for faith having to do with driving your automobile without knowing for sure that the brakes would always work, something along those lines, he whose sedan was perpetually low on brake fluid, wiper fluid, transmission fluid, as he hurtled from hospital to hospital to comfort the sick and the dying. He racked his brain to make the whole business accessible to her, like Jesus with his simple but inscrutable parables, but what he hadn't known was that her car had become her worst enemy, that she never knew whether or not she'd be able to make it to the shoulder when the flash of fear came over her and her arms stiffened, elbows locked as she tried to force herself to the roadside without sideswiping another vehicle.

She felt a rage toward God like she'd never felt toward anyone, for not existing, for making a dupe of her father, one more name to add to the growing genealogy of victims, as if there hadn't been enough sacrifices already to appease his prurient bloodthirsty idle curiosity at the scene of the accident after some anonymous person's brakes had failed unexpectedly, enough sacrifices to redeem the whole of humanity many times over.

Let God have a few panic attacks, let him try it, three or four would suffice, and then afterward go lie down in green pastures by still waters the way she'd lain in the middle of the field beyond the irrigation ditch figuring out how to get to her feet and back to the car she'd abandoned several hundred feet away, with the buzzer going off to remind her she'd left the keys in the ignition and the door open on the driver's side. Let him attempt the ultimate suicide, deicide, and then try to go back and look upon the wonder of his creation. He couldn't look back that way, any more than her, because even if he came out of his depressed omniscient stupor long enough to convince himself that performing the miracle of curing himself wasn't totally pointless, he still wouldn't be able to recover his innocence. You couldn't attempt to destroy yourself and return afterward to being fully godlike, never again, because even if you botched the job and survived, the memory alone of your deep and impetuous self-hatred would poison your every act from then on, world without end. She wanted an explanation right now, right this very second, of why he had seen fit to give her mind the awesome capacity to turn back on itself with such terrible ferocity that it would do anything, including plotting its own demise, to escape its own thoughts, including the thoughts of plotting its own demise, most especially those.

Let God give himself multiple myeloma, and a bad leg just for kicks, and see how long he continued to believe in himself. He sent Christ as his advance man and suffered by proxy, but that wasn't the same thing, punishing yourself by sacrificing your son. He was getting off on the technicality that he contained everything. She called him a charlatan to his face, an egomaniac, a callous shithead, every epithet for Yahweh the unspeakable name that crossed her mind; she told him to go fuck himself, to try to provoke him to come out of hiding long enough to prove to one of his insolent creations that he did exist, in spite of anything she might say to the contrary in her bottomless ignorance. She wanted him to strike her stone dead in the back pew of her father's church, kill her in his showoffy, violent, pissant way, so she could at least have the satisfaction for one instant, the instant of her death, of knowing how petty he was, how little he cared, when all was said and done, because he'd entertained himself for millenia by creating humans, giving them an overdose of fear, and letting them cogitate for most of their lives on the fact that no matter what they did or didn't do, no matter how great their striving or their attempts to slow down time, they were moving closer to death at every moment.

Maybe that was how he was punishing her for her sacrilege, by keeping her alive, knowing that although she couldn't quite bring herself to hasten her life's brief parenthesis to its conclusion, it was only a matter of time, whether she did it herself or let natural causes or perhaps a freak accident take care of it. The only difference was the margin for error of a few decades one way or the other. In the final analysis, he remained so indifferent to her case, and her father's, that it didn't much matter whether she or Carson lived to thirty or ninety, because in the infinite consciousness of God, neither sum was anything to get excited about. If she wanted to squander the rest of that time cursing him, that was her own business. Do with it what you will, only try not to spend it all in one place. Most of all she hated him for not existing, and if by some miracle he did indeed exist, then she was doubly fucked for sure.

Her father and the three deacons had returned to the platform, and were singing the invitational hymn. Carson had never been big on proselytizing, he simply wanted to serve the community he was a part of, and he supported the missions of his denomination with reluctance. But he sometimes allowed himself one little Baptist trick, and that was the singing over and over of the last verse of the invitational hymn. If he thought that a member of one of the families of his congregation was close to discovering Christ for himself or herself, then he would put a little heat on by prolonging the baptismal hymn, so the person either had to sweat it out or come to God. Sometimes it gave him a chance to scan his congregation, to look into their faces and hearts one by one and see if there were any stragglers among them. *My body they may kill, but God abideth still.* The guest preacher sat dozing in his chair at the back of the stage. His exertions had worn him out. The four men launched into the fifth and final stanza a second time, as Carson's searching eyes fell now on one pew, now on another.

A sound came from somewhere, a moan, deep and pitiful, filling the small enclosed space of the sanctuary, a sound she wanted to shut her ears against until she realized it was coming from her. Everyone in the pews ahead of her had turned around, every member of the congregation was looking at her, directly at her. Her father's eyes fell on her too, his face fell, and buckling his knees to grope for the cane where he had left it on the seat, he laid his hand on it, lifted himself with a thrust of the cane, and lurched toward the platform stairs. Her pew was filling up with people, all of them reaching out for her, too many hands, too many voices saying urgent words she couldn't understand. They wanted to convert her, they wanted to make her one of their own. With wild jerks of her head, like a bird that has flown into a classroom full of children, she looked for Carson, his Irish nose, his puzzled, grieving, forgiving eyes, but he hadn't been able to push his way through. A chill shook her bones, the onset of a fever, as she tried to fight the interlopers off. There were too many of them, and she was too weak to resist or struggle anymore. As the bodies closed in around her, she sank down into the pew, face pressed against the impermeable wood, and cried, "Daddy, Daddy, don't let me do it."

All she wanted to do was sleep. The sleep wasn't restful, and made her more tired each time she awoke to the darkness and silence, with intermittent cracks of light coming in around the drawn shade. At times, she tried to locate herself within the day by the honking of the geese, but the honking never came, because of course the geese had fled the lake for the season. She knew that, she kept reminding herself of it, but she kept forgetting too, and each time she would experience the same keen disappointment when she remembered that the geese weren't there and then remembered why she was there, and how sad she felt, and how all she wanted to do was sleep because it was the only time she didn't remember anything. Once in a while, her mother brought food, lasagna or orange-juice cake or grilled ribs or cereal, at least that's what her mother said they were, because she couldn't really taste the difference between them, and didn't eat very much of them. Her mother would help her out of bed, force her out of bed actually, long enough to escort her to the bathroom, since even though she held her pee for as long as she could, until her bladder ached the same way the rest of her did, the more so on account of the baby pressing against it, she had to go sometime, and she wouldn't have had any objection to releasing it onto the sheets, and lying in her own stale urine, but she didn't want her mother to have to change the sheets, not so much out of consideration for her mother as because it would mean she'd have to get out of bed anyway, and for a longer time, so she might as well stand up and go to the bathroom.

It was almost too much effort to figure out that not peeing in the bed would allow her to stay under the sheets longer than peeing in the bed would, but somehow she'd managed to make the necessary calculations, if she could only remember them the next time, so she wouldn't have to perform them again. As she sat on the commode with her nightgown hiked up and the door open, blinking in the oppressive and ghastly fluorescent light, her mother's body filling the doorway turned slightly sideways to provide her with a false sense of decorum and privacy, she considered asking about Robbie, whether or not he would be coming back to get her, or at least to visit her, but that also seemed too strenuous a task, to put the question to her mother, especially since follow-up questions would also be required, as her mother had scrupulously avoided mentioning Robbie's name, probably because she thought it would upset her.

But it wouldn't have. To be sad about Robbie, she would have had to differentiate among the causes of her sadness, an impossible task, because she had no idea why she felt so unutterably sad. It was simply a condition of her existence, the primary condition of her existence, and the feeling of sadness had superseded any possible cause and taken on a life of its own, a death in life. All that remained was the cycle of waking and sleep, mostly sleep, though it never seemed enough, and there were dreams too, ones she couldn't remember, only their unpleasant aftertaste and the night sweats they produced. The dreams probably would have been terrifying if she could have remembered them, except that she had been living with terror so long and so intimately, it had graduated chromatically into a chronic numbness.

Her father came to her bedside as often as he could, which wasn't that often, because he tended to be overcome with emotion, and he was afraid that the sight and sound of his tears would bother her, but she was indifferent to everything about his lamentations except their volume. She remembered that feelings were supposed to be attached to them, but they were a curious spectacle, a dumb show with sound. He'd had to sit quietly by so many sickbeds and deathbeds, holding a vigil, he just couldn't remain silent this time. He kept asking her was there anything he could do, anything, anything at all, and she suggested that he say prayers for her, which she knew he was doing anyway, but if the request came from her maybe it would make the prayers seem more efficacious to him, maybe it would expedite them, and would make him feel he could do them anywhere, in his car, in the grocery, in the other room, and then he wouldn't have to come to her room so often.

Some of the times, though, she would groan to indicate that she wanted him or Josie to linger at her bedside a little longer, just to have the cold comfort of another body floating in space with her. Her father would tell her stories about his boyhood and his forebears, to distract her mind, she supposed, but the only one she could remember was one about an ancestor of his, another preacher, who lived in the last century. He'd fallen out with one of his relatives over a well that had been poisoned, because the relative had decided he would rather poison it than share it. Instead of fighting over the well, the preacher vowed that he would find everlasting water another way, so he went into the woods, cut down a black gum tree, hacked off three feet from the hollow of it, then dug down in a dry place where there had never been water before and set the length of gum in it. That evening he knelt and prayed to God to send him and his family everlasting water. The next morning he got up and found no water there, so he knelt down at sunrise and prayed again for drinking water and water for everything he and his kin might need it for. No water came. The next night he knelt down and prayed again for everlasting water. The morning after, when he woke up, the gum was full of good clear water, an abundance of water for all time.

She didn't know what it was supposed to mean, and wasn't

sure what it had to do with her, except something about prayer, but for some reason she could remember the precise details of that story in a less garbled way than she could remember the details of the past few months of her life, which she wanted to forget anyway, so she repeated the story to herself, like a formula, without content, without emotion, without thought, and the repetition helped her to enter more quickly into the domain of sleep. Sleep was the only thing she could imagine might heal her, if it would only stop making her so tired, because if she could sleep for the rest of her life, she would be at peace, or at least she wouldn't know she wasn't at peace, which amounted to the same thing.

The bed she slept in wasn't Lila's. She recalled that Lila's was in storage, somewhere in Lexington, and if she'd had any inkling exactly where, if she'd had enough foresight to go to the storage place to deposit the furniture, instead of leaving it to the boys, she might be able to tell her parents where it was, and they could retrieve it, and at least she'd be able to spend her days and nights in that bed rather than in one that had no meaning to her. When Lila had been dying in that oak bed, the one comfort she'd been able to provide herself with, in the midst of the whole humiliating process, was her belief that she was going to meet Byrd, that they would see each other and be together forever. If her disease hadn't taken such a slow course, she probably never would have become frightened, but the way it lingered on, she had a chance to become disheartened, and that took away the sweetness of her anticipation, to the point that going to meet Byrd became nothing more than a way of saying she was tired of suffering.

Serena didn't think she herself would be able to grow enthused about the prospect of meeting someone in the beyond. Everybody she knew was here, terminally here, and she had nothing to anticipate, unless she could imagine going to join Lila and Byrd, but she didn't relish the prospect of having to tell them about her breakdown, her sex life, the kinds of thoughts she'd been having over the past months. Lila had a knack for knowing when something was on her mind, and she wouldn't let Serena alone until she had come out with it. About the only safe topic among them would be the farm, but then she'd have to go into the details of the bankruptcy, and Byrd would not be able to understand for the life of him why she hadn't planted more than a kitchen garden, hadn't cultivated the acreage, or at least rented out the tobacco part of it.

The Irish mutthound scratched at the door at intervals, whimpering, trying to force it open, then would go away or be dragged away by her mother, until eventually it came back again and did the same thing. After many of these episodes, she told her mother that it was okay, the dog could come in and out as it pleased, she knew that it was used to sleeping under the bed in here, and it didn't make any difference to her, since she was doing the same thing herself. It would be good company because it would be with her but she wouldn't see it. As soon as the door opened, the dog trotted across the throw rug and squeezed itself underneath the bed. She watched its hind legs and tail disappear.

That afternoon, with her father probably in his study at church, the house was silent except for the occasional bang of the cuckoo clock in the living room and the almost silent shufflings of her mother doing housework to create the illusion that she remained indoors all day long because there were things to do, and not because she was afraid to leave Serena in the house by herself for even a moment, in case she shook off her lethargy long enough to make the arduous pilgrimage across the living room to the silverware drawer in the kitchen or the medicine cabinet in the bathroom, although Serena was sure that any offending items had been discreetly removed and placed in an undisclosed location.

In the expansive near-silence, Jake began to thrash and make assorted soulful doggie noises while he whacked his tail against the bottom of the mattress and turned himself over and over, looking for a comfortable position. There was nothing remarkable about the noises except that she realized she was making a mental catalogue of them, distinguishing them by the degree of interest or annoyance they were causing her. Then she realized that she had been having actual thoughts, ones about her grandmother and Byrd, and that her awareness of the house had gradually expanded to the point where she could contain all of its space in her mind, and she could ascertain the comings and goings of Carson and Josie, and knew which part of the house they were in at all times, and the arrival of Carson's gargantuan automobile was starting to become predictable. She could hear its approach at various times of the day as he returned from errands or work, the rattle of the sticking valve becoming audible a few seconds before it reached the long uphill driveway, then the roar of the engine as he floored it, and the sound gradually moved around the house until it vibrated only a few feet from her bed, on the other side of the wall. He always returned at least twice during the day, once in late morning, the other about an hour before dinnertime.

Sliding back the sheet, she sat up and eased her legs around until they touched the floor. After testing their ability to support her, she stood, woozy, and floated to the doorknob. She opened the door. The mutthound came out from under the bed at once, and followed her into the living room, in case he might miss something important. Her mother, a dishtowel over her arm, was rearranging fruit in a ceramic bowl, pears, apples, bananas, and kiwi fruit. She always said that having fresh fruit out on the table was one of the things that made life worth living. Josie tried not to betray her surprise, by switching the places of an apple and a pear. "I've gotta pee," Serena mumbled. Then, as an afterthought, she said, "I think after that I might go sit in the sunroom for a few minutes. Could you fix me a glass of cranberry juice?"

That evening, Carson brought Rusty, her grandfather, back to the house with him. Her grandfather was pushing eighty, and his world was simple and defined, not because he was senile—he wasn't—but because his world had always been that way. It was a world in which women cooked and gave birth, men worked and talked about county politics while they pitched horseshoes, and everyone worshipped. Whenever something bad happened, whether it was to him or someone else, his favorite expression was "God's will be done." She envied him that world. Whenever he talked of it, it seemed like some mythic country that could never really exist. Some of the people around him had begun to treat him like a character, because he had aged, even though he did and said many of the same things as in his younger days. But he had the last laugh, because he was oblivious to their condescension. He worked in his garden, complimented pretty women on their legs, and watched the evening news without absorbing any of its catastrophic commentary about the state of things. His body had turned out to be more sturdy than his son's, and he was always hauling big containers of dirt around. He had the same Irish looks as Serena and her father, only closer to the source.

She saw them turn into the driveway from her perch on the sunroom sofa, where she had been contemplating twigs sheathed in ice, and the patches of lake visible among the bare branches. His arrival brought her a fleeting sensation of happiness, enough to bring her to her feet to meet him at the back door. She gave him a hug. His wool coat, dusted with snow, smelled of the outdoors. "Hi, Grandpa."

"That's the nicest squeeze I've had all day. You get prettier every time I see you. I believe you've changed your hair again. You girls have more hairdos than I do neckties."

"You don't own any neckties. I've never seen you wear one."

"Well, if I did, then. There's a terrible smell coming from around the garden beds out there, and it's not horse manure either. I know a right smart about what that smells like."

"I think they're mothballs. Mom sprinkles them around to keep the dogs from digging the tulip bulbs up in the winter."

"This place gets wilder every time I see it. You got to get your momma and daddy to cut down some of the trees. One of the big windstorms we're always getting is going to cave the roof in.

Here, take this sack of hot peppers to Josie. I planted those last summer by mistake, and my freezer is full of them."

She told her mother that she would dress and come to the table for supper. Her mother nodded without making any comment, but Serena could see her face lighten a little, and she became conscious of the tremendous strain her mother was under. She reached out and stroked Josie's aging cheek. "If there are angels in heaven, Mom, you're going to be among them." Her mother, the pagan, fought back tears. That night at dinner, her grandfather was in fine form. He told gossip and anecdotes nonstop with his mouth full of brisket as he sliced haphazardly at the meat.

"Those peppers is spicy, now. I had one with my eggs this morning and it like to took off the top of my head. You need to try one, son. They're full of Vitamin C and I read somewheres that's supposed to be good for cancer. It can't hurt, anyway. Serena, did I tell you about two fellows my great-great-grandpappy knew, before they came over on the boat? Two Irishmen they were, traveling along the road in Ireland, and had worked up an appetite from the walking. Come up on a garden with a stone wall around it, and John says, 'What is them pretty red things over there?' Pat says to John, 'Looks like cherries to me, and ready for picking. I'm a-going to climb over and have a mouthful or two.' He snatched a handful, popped them in his mouth and went to chawing. Next thing you know, he was weeping, boo hoo hoo, and John says, he says, 'Whatever on airth are ye crying about?' Pat said, 'Fat to my Christ'—excuse me about the strong language, son, but I got to tell it the way it happened. Says, 'Fat to my Christ, I'm crying because my pappy done died and never tasted none of these good cherries here.' Well, John says, 'If they're that good, why, I believe I'll have me a nibble.' So over the stone wall he goes too, and pulled off seven or eight, and popped them in his mouth. The tears, they come streaming down his face. 'What are you crying about?' Pat asks him. And John says, 'I'm crying because you didn't die before your father did.'"

"You're always good for tattling on some wicked Irishmen," said Carson. He was working on his second helping of scalloped potatoes. Serena knew he didn't have any real appetite on account of the nausea produced by his oral chemotherapy. But he ate anyway, trusting that if he performed the gesture of eating, the appetite would follow. Carson had gained back almost all of the thirty pounds he'd lost at the beginning, and she couldn't detect even a trace of bitterness in him, though she was always on the lookout for it. She had been pushing the brisket around her plate, and with a great effort, lifted a bite of it to her mouth and let it dissolve there.

"We're so ornery, there's plenty to tell on us. So, sugar, how have you been this last little while? I heared tell you had got into the farming line, and you haven't yet been over to see your grandpappy and ask his advice about crops. You should have seen my tomatoes last summer. They was so big I saved one and used it as a jack-o-lantern at Halloween."

"Well, we tried farming as an experiment, but we decided it wasn't going to work as well as we thought."

"I hear that. It's not for everybody. The way they play around with the price supports so much, it's a wonder anybody can make a go of it today. If what they charge me for my fertilizer at the hardware store is any indication, I'm not surprised you gave it up. But the Lord's been good to me. I've got my health, except for some prostate trouble, and I live in my own house, and I get my pension check every month from where I worked at the steel mills up in Ohio. Although it ain't anything to write home about. I can't afford those good cuts of meat like Josie and Carson eats over here. I eat lower on the hog. So what's your plan now, sugar? I won't tell you to get a husband and kids, because I know you're too grownup for that. Are you taking a little vacation with your folks before you go back to acting on Broadway?"

"I never did work on Broadway, Grandpa. It was off-off Broadway, and I did the technical end. Kelsey's the actress."

"On Broadway, off Broadway, it's all the same to me. I never go to the theater anyway. I tried the Dinner Barn off Sixty-four a couple of times, but with my hearing aid turned up, all I could hear was the silverware."

"I'm staying here with Mom and Dad for a while. It's been a hard few months, and I need to rest before I go back to work."

"That's it. You rest, honey. You do look a little peakéd. I can't hardly sleep more than two or three hours any more myself, but I think young people should be well rested because their lives are so busy. When you get all rested, I want you to come over to Mount Sterling and read to me out of my Bible one day. Carson got me a large print version, but I still can't see the letters. They don't make the print big enough, if the truth be told."

"I will, Grandpa."

"Your daddy has got me as a captive audience for his sermons all this winter, but come next summer, I plan to skip a few Sundays and do a little worship in my garden." He gave her a conspicuous wink. "Don't tell Carson, but I'm a nature worshipper. I only go to Bethel because they serve coffee cake downstairs before the service."

"Don't worry. I won't tell."

After dinner, she volunteered to clean up, while her parents and her grandfather repaired to the living room. Washing the dishes gave her a peculiar pleasure, the hot suds between her hands, the way it made the dishes feel slick, melting the grease on contact; then she rinsed it away and placed each dish in the drainer to air dry. The order and simplicity of the task allowed her to stop thinking for a few minutes. Otherwise, each time her mind started to achieve a momentary serenity, she would remember she was depressed, that she had wanted to kill herself, that Robbie was gone, that she was bankrupt and hated herself, and the heavy throb would permeate her brain again, making it impossible to experience a respite for long. If someone would only stand next to her for the rest of her life, handing her dishes to wash, the finite objects of an infinite task, she thought she would be able to get by.

The next morning, she awoke early, and dressed before lethargy had a chance to paralyze her. The sky continued gray, but a glow smoldered behind it, giving the massed clouds a metallic hue. When she tiptoed through the living room so as not to wake her mother, and put a single piece of toast, the heel, her favorite part of the loaf, into the toaster, she heard her mother stir in the bedroom. The clothes hook on her and Carson's bedroom door made it impossible to close the door all the way, so it always remained open a crack. Her mother's feet hit the floor hard, and the clothes hook twanged as she pulled her bathrobe off it in a hurry. Once she was in the living room and saw Serena sitting quietly at the table, eating a piece of toast smeared with apple butter, her movement slowed, and she tried to be casual.

"I tossed and turned all night, between my sinuses and the wind beating the shingles. I'm going to make some coffee so my rear won't be dragging the ground all morning." Her hands went to work, spreading the filter, pouring the ground coffee, filling the carafe. "You want some?"

"Sure." Serena turned her attention to the long trough outside the window, the bottom lined with a thin layer of birdseed. "Do you keep that going all winter?"

"I do. Most of the birds have scatted until spring, but the squirrels still come around. I call it my squirrel feeder. I need to get out there and refill, but it's been too cold."

"Mom, you don't have to keep a constant eye on me. If I plan to do myself in, I promise I'll give notice first."

"Don't talk that way. I'm not keeping an eye on anybody," said Josie, her voice filled with mock indignation. "I have to get some coffee in me before I turn into an ogre. I'm allowed in my own kitchen, aren't I? The old man's in there doing so much carpentry I'll never get back to sleep anyway."

"I'm going to take a walk around Chalk Lake this morning, and get a little air."

"Let me throw some slacks on and I'll go with you. The coffee won't take a minute."

"I told you, I'm okay this morning. I just feel incredibly shitty and miserable, which is an improvement over what I was. Jake can keep me company. He needs the exercise."

As soon as Jake heard her speak his name, he began to pace,

toenails clacking along the hardwood. "All right, honey," Josie answered, her voice tentative. "I'll be right here when you get back. You said you lost your gloves. There's an extra pair in the closet. Somebody walked off and left them here last year."

Outside, blue shadows, their edges indistinct, had been laid down by the trees and houses. Her eyes teared from the cold, and she wiped them with her muffler. She liked the smell of the damp wool. Jake romped in the snow, making porpoise jumps. A man wearing a tartan hat and earmuffs was shoveling around a mailbox, and he waved to her. When she got closer, she recognized him as the caretaker.

"Cold enough for you?"

"It feels pretty good," she said. "My lungs ache a little, but it wakes me up."

"Lordy, I wish I was still in bed. This starting my day at four thirty is for the birds, but if I don't get the bad patches cleared off the road, and shovel around the mailboxes of the few of you that's out here in the wintertime, there won't be any mail today."

"That's nice of you to do that."

"It ain't nice, it's my job."

"Your name's Hank, isn't it?"

"Yep, last I heard. Why, somebody have another job for me? I won't be able to get to it until I'm done here."

"No, I just wanted to see you."

"About what?"

"About nothing. I knew that once I saw you, I'd remember your name."

He looked puzzled. "Well, now you seen me. You and the pup out for a walk?"

"We thought we'd go around the lake."

"You won't get far back toward the main highway, with the snow the way it is, but if you traipse this other direction, you can walk halfway around and double back. That Jake of yours is a rascal. He's got a girlfriend in every other house in the summertime. A regular gigolo, he is. Aren't you, Jake? He must get pretty lonesome this time of year."

"Not too lonesome. He's got me. Only I make him sleep under the bed instead of in it."

"My wife does me the same way. You all have a nice walk, now, and watch the ice on the bridge."

When she reached the bridge, which had no guard rail, she stopped to survey the water. Small, incessant waves lapped at the pebbles, and she coud hear a hollow, sucking sound as the water sluiced back into the tide. The lake seemed animate, actively mocking her tentative resolve. She wondered whether she would ever be able to see it again as just a lake, or whether it would have a malevolent aspect from now on. "You're not going to scare me," she shouted, and her words echoed over the lake in the frozen air. Jake flinched, as if she had threatened him with a newspaper. Removing one glove, she stooped to scratch the underside of his chin, and he licked her hand all over, the warm breath from his nostrils steaming upward in a vapor. Come summer, she would swim here again, and bring her father down to the pier with her so he could watch, get over his nervousness, enjoy the spectacle of her body moving strong through the water, then she'd climb out, and come up behind him to soak his shirt with water when she hugged him.

Then she remembered that she would have an infant by then. If she didn't marry Robbie, and stayed on with her parents, she would become an unwed mother, a jezebel, like the prematurely hard, spindly, redheaded teenager with splotches of freckles down her arms in the trailer park that was starting to form at the entrance of the road to Chalk Lake. As far as the citizens of this county were concerned, there were no single mothers, only unwed ones, the ones who were always the villains in the welfare stories. No one would ever reprimand her openly, or exclude her from any activities, mainly because of the regard in which they held Carson. Nonetheless, she would be a pariah to them.

Once, when she passed by the encampment of trailers in good weather, she had spied the freckled teenager walking about the hardscrabble yard quickly and tensely with a baby in her arms, as if she were handling a hot casserole dish without the benefit of potholders, and looking for a stump to set it down on before she raised blisters on her hands. But the teenager never would set the baby down, as she passed from her nonexistent adolescence straight into a truncated adulthood. The girl knew beforehand that all her born days would be hard and miserable, a short life of trouble. Yet she hung on like grim death, on the off-chance that things might turn out otherwise, knowing that the odds were tremendously against it.

Serena used to think of that trailer park clan, with their broken-down trucks and clotheslines, their sallow, pasty, tattooed men forever hauling junk back and forth, as rednecks and eyesores. But they didn't seem like rednecks or eyesores to her anymore. The existence of the baby within her, she knew, was already turning into a solace of sorts. She was beginning to understand why those perpetually underfed women would let a baby suck the last drop of life out of them, if necessary, rather than give it up. She knew that she wasn't going to deliberately, physically harm herself, not because she felt any particular happiness or cared that much right now about her future, but because to destroy herself would also be to destroy the baby. Whether that counted as optimism or just a dumb biological imperative, she couldn't say.

Jake wallowed in the snow, flaunting his thick winter coat. When he had thoroughly covered himself with a dusting of white, he trotted back over to her and gave himself a vigorous shake. He stared at her, ears pricked, muzzle slack, in his trusting doggie way, fully expecting that she would take him on a longer walk than to the bridge and back. The fact that she had once kneed him in the throat under the table, in her impatience, because his breath was bad and because he had drunk from the toilet, didn't count for anything with him. He probably didn't even remember the incident, and if he did, it was neither more nor less than what he expected.

Racing ahead with his head lowered, he barked like mad at nothing, or at something only he could hear in the brightening air of a winter morning.

She was doing a crossword puzzle, trying to think of a five-letter word for "pre-Columbian abacus." As much as she had always loved to work crosswords, she wasn't particularly skilled at them, and she simply left blank the items she couldn't figure out, without searching through dictionaries or other source books. The fact that most of the terms in the puzzle were arcane and esoteric appealed to her, and it didn't bother her that she usually couldn't fill more than half the spaces. Sometimes, if she sat fretting over the clue long enough, or simply moved on to the next one, the word would come to her. Often, it was a word she hadn't even known that she knew. Though the cabin was cluttered with stacks and boxes of her father's books, mostly theology and philosophy, the idea of reading to fill her empty hours hadn't appealed to her. But when Carson brought her home a crossword magazine from the grocery store, which she found stuck in the bag between a stalk of celery and a carton of eggs while putting the groceries away, she felt an immediate urge to curl up in a chair and start working one.

Though Serena had failed to show up at the day-care center without giving notice, for however many days had passed, Josie had explained to Stefano that her daughter was going through a bad time, without elaborating, and Stefano said he would try to hold the job for her, or at least make hours available to her when she was ready.

Quipu. The word fit the *i* and the *u* she'd already figured out from horizontal words. Even though she wasn't going to check a reference source, if she could even find one for such a thing, she let the word stand. *Quipu.* It didn't look familiar to her, even after she'd written it down in the spaces, but it felt like the right word, and in any case, there were other spaces to complete. The vertical words were always the hardest, it seemed to her. Whether that was by design of the anonymous person who made up the puzzle, or simply because it was harder to think up to down rather than left to right, she wasn't sure. But she took a mild satisfaction in watching the grid start to fill with scrawls of lead pencil.

The phone rang, and Josie, who was peeling potatoes, said she'd answer it. Picking up the receiver, she stood listening and saying noncommital things like "Uh-huh," and "I see." Then, putting her hand over the receiver, she said, sotto voce, "It's Robbie. Are you up to talking?" A little evanescent thrill went through her, and she nodded and took the phone. Her mother returned to the kitchen and turned on the radio, to manufacture some privacy in the small cabin.

"Hello?"

"Hi, Serena. I'm, you know, glad you're up and around. I hope you're not too bored out there on the lake."

"Where are you? Vail?"

"Nah, I came back from Colorado a couple of nights after, you know, after your parents called Matt, because they didn't know where I was, and he called the Forest Service, and a couple of rangers hiked up into the backcountry and found me in a little snow house I'd made."

"You mean a couple of nights after I almost killed myself."

"That's what I meant. It's hard for me to say it. I can't say I really understand. I never could imagine that you'd do it. But you didn't, and I'm happy about that, babe, you don't know how awful I would have felt. Not that it matters how I feel. But before the rangers came, I was walking around in the middle of the forest, and the sky had cleared off, it was crystal clear, so I was stargazing, you know, like I always do. Except that I forgot my star chart. But I know a lot of them anyway, and even though I'm kind of an agnostic I guess you would call it, I was throwing out prayers to Cassieopia, and the Pleiades, all those Greek ones, and I really felt like things were going to turn out okay for us."

"Why haven't you been to see me?" She tried not to make the question sound like an accusation. There was nothing to accuse him of, except self-preservation.

"I wanted to come, you know, I got a flight straight back, a redeye, and I was planning on bringing you some Joe Bologna's pizza from Lexington, with those awesome garlic bread sticks, because your Mom said you didn't have much appetite, but then she told me you were sleeping a lot, and she didn't think you were up to talking to me. So I waited." He fell silent. "I hope I didn't wait too long."

"I am pleased you called. I would say happy, but it's hard for me to feel happy about anything right now. Everything is kind of flat."

"Listen, I know I was pretty crabby after I messed my knee up, and I really do apologize for that. Sometimes I don't know how to act in tense situations. I went stir crazy. I'm trying to grow up, it just takes time."

"What happened to me doesn't have anything to do with you, Robbie. At least no more than it has to do with anything else. I can't even figure out what's wrong with me. If anything, I have to apologize to you for getting pregnant without your consent."

"Look, forget it. You're bummed out enough without laying that shit on top of it."

"Shall I tell you something? I know it complicates things, but conceiving is the only part of my life that hasn't been a mistake."

"Now you're talking. That baby is going to be awesome. Dweezil if it's a boy, Moon Unit if it's a girl. All I want is to see you. Do you want all vegetarian, or can I get sausage on half of it?"

She laughed in spite of herself. "I don't think there's anybody quite like you, Robbie. Come out for a visit, and let's see where things stand. But Robbie?"

"Yeah, babe."

"About the sex, I don't think I'll be up to it for a while. It's not because I don't care for you."

"Don't sweat it. I can jerk off."

"Oh. Well, I suppose you could."

"I'm only joking. It's good to hear you laugh, and I was trying to keep it going. My jokes aren't so hot, though."

"No, I think it's because my sense of humor has ossified, along with everything else. I'm afraid I'm not going to be much fun for a while."

"That's no biggie either. Matt's no fun either, and I been putting up with his ass for twenty years now."

"You're sweet. You know that I do love you, don't you? I want you to remember that, even if it doesn't look much like it sometimes. It wasn't you that I wanted to get away from."

"I wasn't sure that you did love me, actually. When I got above the tree line, I couldn't tell whether or not I would come back. I'm glad to hear you speak the words. If you say it's true, I'm not going to question it."

"Come tomorrow morning."

"I'll be there. I'll make it all vegetarian, in case you're hungry."

She agreed to try a psychiatrist. The woman, whose name was Fran, looked unprepossessing. She was short, middle-aged, rotund, bespectacled, had no chin, and seemed slightly ill at ease in her dress. Serena liked her instantly.

Fran began the session by telling Serena a little about herself. She had lived with the nuns of an order so small it bordered on extinction. For several years, she had participated in their activities as a novice, until the time came for her to decide whether or not to take her final vows, then she left the order. Mostly, she had simply grown weary of living among elderly nuns who all seemed complaisant and sure of their places in heaven. Also, she felt she was getting too far away from the world. She decided she was either going to teach literacy in the prisons, or become a psychiatrist. She spoke as though there were an obvious connection between the two things. It hadn't been necessary for Fran to tell Serena anything about herself, but perhaps she was used to going to confession, and felt it would be dishonest to hide her religious past.

Fran didn't seem much inclined toward humor. In fact, she looked a bit careworn, as if she could use a laugh from someone else. Nonetheless, she tried to put Serena more at ease about the situation by quipping that she didn't know if she could make her feel better, but she promised to save her immortal soul. "Good," said Serena. "That's what I'm here for."

Fran was a bit discombobulated by the reply, since Serena wasn't smiling, but she let it pass. Then Serena began to talk, and didn't stop until the hour was over. She cried uncontrollably most of the time, so that it was difficult to enunciate her words. Half the time, she didn't know whether Fran could understand what she was saying, or whether she was simply communicating to her in a primal language. She talked nonstop about death, depression, suicide, sex, as if someone deranged held a gun to her head, and she were trying to tell him all the reasons why he shouldn't kill her, knowing all the while that as soon as she took a breath he was going to pull the trigger anyway.

Fran mostly limited herself to yanking tissues out of the box and handing them to Serena. Then, when Serena had depleted herself, and it was time for her to leave, Fran said, "You know, you're way ahead of me in one respect. It was only a couple of years ago that it really sunk in for me that I was going to die some day. Most of those nuns in the order's apartment house were about a hundred and thirty, you see, the way the people are in the Old Testament, and I was afraid the same thing was going to happen to me." She gave Serena something close to a smile, probably as close as she could manage, and Serena knew she would come back.

Her father sat in the sunroom on the sofa, wearing his bifocals and staring down into passages of Greek, which to Serena looked like a field of mathematical symbols. The radio had said the wind chill factor was twenty below zero, which was difficult to fathom, after she'd spent so many years hearing the actual temperature without regard to any other variables. The thick panes of glass in the sunroom, despite the cold, made the rays falling onto her father's hair and across the wall feel warm. He liked to sit in the sunroom because it gave him a spectacular view of the lake, and now that he couldn't swim in it anymore, he spent a lot of time contemplating it through Josie's indoor foliage. The surface appeared to have frozen over. She couldn't remember her parents speaking of that ever having happened before. Maybe it was the first time on record. Given how new Chalk Lake was, in comparison to the rest of the earth, that seemed eminently possible.

The book in her father's hands was probably something of a religious nature, an obscure commentary on one of the books of the Bible, but she knew that wasn't why he read it. It gave him the same kind of pleasure that she derived from working crossword puzzles. Sitting down next to Carson on the couch, she asked him to read aloud to her, and he began to give her a halting translation of its content. "No," she said. "I just want to hear the sounds." So he began to speak aloud in a foreign tongue, and she closed her eyes so there would be no distractions to the round and gentle cadences of his voice. Robbie would be here in an hour or two, and Kelsey would arrive at the airport tomorrow.

She hadn't wanted Kelsey to come so soon, especially since she'd have to take out a loan to pay for her own ticket, but she knew her sister too well to think that a wish of hers could have any impact on Kelsey's decision. "Remember, you're fucked in the head," Kelsey had said to her over the phone, "which means you've abdicated all power of veto to me. So I'm coming to Kentucky." "You know," said Serena, "you're *soooo* lucky to be born in Kentucky where the girls are so plucky." Kelsey was ready with the usual retort. "Oh, yeah? Well, that's Devra with a vee to you." In their burst of familiar laughter, they could pretend for a moment that nothing had happened. After Kelsey arrived, there would be a lot of weeping, and they would have to abandon the pretense that everything was the same. Serena knew that at any moment, the terror could rise up in her again as strong as it had ever been. All Kelsey wanted for now was something recognizable to hold onto over the phone until she could see her sister in the flesh.

Serena could hear her mother in the kitchen humming a song as she put away dishes. She recognized the tune as one that Josie often went around singing, that started off "How many biscuits can you eat this morning?" and then said something like "Forty-nine and a ham of meat." It had never been clear to Serena how much meat was in a ham of meat, but then again, she'd never bothered to ask, because the phrase seemed to fit with the song. She started to feel drowsy from the sunlight through the glass, which had made its way over to her. It was not the kind of torpor that preceded a fall into the abyss, but instead, something akin to the drowsiness she had experienced regularly as a child. Her first instinct was to curl up and put her head in her father's lap, but she remembered that his bad leg would also go to sleep if she did, from the pressure of her head, so that wasn't something she'd be able to do any more, at least not for more than a minute. Still, she knew that if she had dozed off in that position, her father wouldn't have disturbed her by trying to get up, and that knowledge alone gave her some comfort.

She remembered a story he sometimes told at the breakfast table, about how when she had been an infant, he had gotten up one night to quiet her colic, and after walking around with her in his arms for a while, he was so groggy that he had sat down in one of the easy chairs, put his legs together, placed her in the impromptu cradle they made, and closed his eyes to rest them for a second. When he opened his eyes again, it was the next morning, and his legs were completely numb from the waist down, but somehow he hadn't let them open. Serena was still there, nestled between them, in slumber. Josie inevitably would roll her eyes when he told the anecdote. "Here goes the old codger again, regaling the multitudes with his minor miracles. I swear, preacher man, would you just go ahead and walk on water and get it over with?" "All right, all right," Carson would answer. "That's exactly what I plan to do, right after I've eaten my other forty-six biscuits and my ham of meat. I'm only up to three biscuits so far. Pass me the basket."

A Kentucky native, Johnny Payne grew up in Lexington, which serves as locus for this novel and a novel-in-progress, *Kentuckiana*.

He received the M. F. A. from the University of Alabama and, from Stanford University, the Ph. D. in English and Comparative Literature. For extended periods, he has lived in Peru, where he researched regional literature and oral tradition. A considerable portion of his work thus centers upon Latin American literature, and includes *Conquest of the New Word: Experimental Fiction & Translation in the Americas* (Univ. of Texas, 1993); a collection of Peruvian folklore, *The She-Calf & Other Quechua Folk Tales* (Univ. of New Mexico, in press); and *The Ambassador's Son*, a novella of modern-day Peru. His writing has appeared in *Southern Review*, *Triquarterly*, and numerous other journals and quarterlies. A musical play, *The Devil in Disputanta*, co-written with composer William Underwood, is based on the family lore of his Appalachian forebears.

He lives with his wife, Miriam, and two children in Evanston, Illinois, where he teaches writing at Northwestern University.